Two-Lane Blacktop

by

Gary Ader

Published in the United States of America by
Escarpment Press, Indian Land, SC

www.escarpmentpress.weebly.com
INDIAN LAND, SC

Dedication

In loving memory of Judy: wife, lover, best friend for 52 years. Her encouragement and guidance made this work possible.

Chapter 1

"What?" Ray shouted.

He was alone in the car and hit the brakes hard, as he veered into the next turnout of the country road. The dust plume behind his car overtook him as he came to a stop.

His daughter, Jennifer, had called him from the airport. She was boarding a flight to Paris. Her final words, before her usual, "Love ya, bye," were, "Regards from Oscar."

How the hell does she know Oscar?

His foot pressed so hard on the brake pedal; the muscles in his calf began to quiver. By now, Jennifer was airborne, and he would have to wait until she arrived in Paris to call her.

He was on his way to pick up some odds and ends from Home Depot and planned to stop at the supermarket for something easy to make for dinner. Neither stop seemed important now. Checking the narrow road for traffic, he turned the SUV back toward home. He had things to do.

Gary Ader

Chapter 2

Ray Walker was a respected businessman and family man. That was the side of him everyone knew. But he had another side, one only a few people knew about. For over fifty years, he had led a secret life as a spy. Recruited as a teenager, during the darkest days of the Cold War, he was an agent of the Culper Ring, a secret spy network that reported directly to the sitting President of the United States. Formed by George Washington during the War of Independence from Britain, this organization, unknown to the other intelligence agencies, has endured until the present day.

All of the agents Ray had worked with had passed away, except for his handler, Olivia Sarah Carr, code named Oscar. He hadn't had any communication with her in years, and assumed she too had retired. How did his daughter Jennifer get mixed up in all of this and why? Did Maurice have anything to do with it?

Ray remembered his last trip to Paris many years before. The now white hairs on the back of his neck stood up as he recalled the danger he had been in. A young French woman, working for the East German Stazi spy organization was determined to intercept an important message he had received for the president, and she and her associates were planning to kill him to get it. Going beyond any training he had received, and without authorization, he killed her to save himself and complete his mission.

It was the one and only time he had taken a life, and for over forty years he had devised elaborate rationalizations to justify his action. He had many other missions, or "adventures," as he liked to call them, and only a few had been as dangerous as the situation he faced in Paris. Even his mission to Moscow to smuggle out the location of a Soviet submarine that had sunk off the coast of Norway, was not as frightening as his mission to Paris.

Now, his daughter was flying there on what must be a mission for Oscar and the Culper Ring. He felt the fear in his gut all over again, only worse, now that it was his child who was in harm's way. His fear quickly turned to anger. He still remembered Olivia's phone number and he dialed it.

"Hello," a familiar female voice answered.

"This is Suitcase," Ray said, using an outdated recognition code.

She hesitated. "This is Oscar."

"One-five-zero." Ray used the confirmation code.

"Two-zero-five. Ray what the hell is going on?"

"You tell *me* what the hell is going on. My daughter called me from the airport, before boarding a flight to Paris, and the last thing she said was, 'Regards from Oscar.' "

"Ray, don't get excited. I can explain."

"You're going to have a lot to explain. Do you remember my trip to Paris?"

"Yes, I remember, but this is different. It's nothing like—"

"Where are you?" he interrupted.

"I'm home in Washington. Why?" she answered hesitantly.

"I'll be there tomorrow, midday, and you're going to tell me how my daughter became involved in this."

"Ray, your parents never knew," she protested.

"Olivia, we've known each other more than fifty years. I think you owe me some fucking professional courtesy here."

"You know how we work. There are no professional courtesies, only the mission," she snapped.

"Screw the mission. We'll talk about this tomorrow, and you had better make sure nothing happens to my daughter." He tried to keep from shouting.

"Yes, of course. She will be all right, but you won't be able to get a flight. There's a storm up here and all flights are cancelled."

Olivia knew how strong-willed Ray was, and hoped delaying their confrontation would give him time to cool down. But he was stubborn, like her, and maybe that was a good thing. He had always completed his missions, no matter what the cost.

He handled things his own way, and not always according to procedure. Some members of the Central Committee were concerned his luck would run out one day, and a mission could be jeopardized, or another asset put at risk. The only reason he was never officially called on the carpet was because of his steadfast loyalty.

During the days of the Cold War he was sent to Moscow to obtain information and smuggle it back to the West. He was new to the spy business, and a trip behind enemy lines was more dangerous than he realized. As it turned out, his inexperience was his biggest asset. Simply put, he had no idea how much danger he was in. He was just an ordinary guy doing ordinary things. A more experienced agent might have been too cautious and aroused suspicion. Now, he was compelled by another imperative: the safety of his daughter.

"Then I'll drive up," he told Olivia. "I'll be there at noon tomorrow."

"Ray, why don't you wait a few days? The storm will pass, and we can plan to meet then. Maybe I can meet you halfway or something."

"See you at noon tomorrow," Ray insisted. "I know the address."

"Very well, we'll talk then. Have a safe trip," she said coldly.

Ray first met Olivia when he was thirteen and she was nineteen. It wasn't until almost a decade later that they had actually gotten to know each other. Over the half-century that followed, they worked together and developed a strong respect and affection for one another.

Now things were different. In Ray's mind she had crossed a line. In Olivia's mind, Ray was failing to see the similarities in the way he, and now his daughter Jennifer, had become a part of the Culper Ring. It never occurred to him that his daughter possessed the same patriotic passion that had driven him. Whether it was by genetic predisposition, or from an upbringing that nurtured those feelings, Ray would never know.

Chapter 3

Ray's wife, Wendy, was visiting a friend in Florida. He called her to tell her he would be driving up to Washington to visit an old friend.

"I should be back in two or three days. I love you," he said.

"I love you too. Drive carefully. I hear they're having some awful weather up there."

He could tell from her voice that she missed him. He missed her too, but now his concern for their daughter outweighed all other feelings.

Ray literally threw some clothes into a suitcase. He packed his shaving bag, laptop, and a bottle of scotch in a duffel.

He put his bags in the back of his SUV, and it was just after three in the afternoon when he got on the road. He planned on making it as far as Richmond, Virginia that night. In the morning, after rush hour, he would head to Olivia's house in Washington, and estimated he would arrive very close to noon, even if the weather were bad.

From Hendersonville, North Carolina, he drove to Asheville and took I-40 east. It was mostly sunny and seasonally cool on this autumn day in the mountains. His mind ran in circles trying to understand. He wondered what kind of danger his daughter might be getting into. Stazi had long since been replaced by the FSB. He tried hard to contain his anger. Learning that Olivia had somehow recruited his daughter into the espionage business was a shock. How could he have been so oblivious? How could he not have noticed any telltale signs from things she said, her attitude, or demeanor?

Wait! he thought. *Jennifer said she was going to see Maurice. Is that the key?*

Maurice was Abby's son. Ray met Abby in college, and she, too, was an agent for the Culper Ring, and had been killed on a mission in Geneva back in the eighties. Jennifer and Maurice met when they were kids at a holiday party. They were pen pals since the days before e-mail.

Why didn't they tell me? Did they think I couldn't handle it?

Actually, Olivia and Jennifer *knew* he couldn't handle it, and they knew if he ever found out, he would do exactly what he was doing now: going absolutely bat-shit crazy.

At Durham, Ray turned on to I-85, which ran northeast to intersect I-95 at Petersburg, Virginia, about fifty miles south of Richmond.

It was after five now, and daylight started to fade. He could see high cirrus clouds moving toward him from the north. His thoughts turned to Jennifer. She would be arriving in Paris in a few hours. It was the memory of his trip to Paris that was the cause of his stress. He thought to himself that if Jennifer were flying to Rome and had said, "regards from Oscar" he probably would not have been so upset.

"Bullshit!" he said aloud

The miles rolled by, and daylight faded to a dim glow to his left.

He remembered the evening in Paris when he walked with Natalie past the *Place de l'Opera*, and through the side streets of Paris to the Seine. That's where it happened. Natalie kept asking for the envelope a French spy had passed to him. She even offered him sex if he would give it to her.

Natalie was working for Stasi, the brutal East German equivalent of the CIA. She was determined to do whatever was necessary to get the information. Ray was willing to protect it with his life if he had to. But that was his second choice. His first choice, the one he made, was to take hers.

Standing in the shadows on the bank of the Seine he kissed her, and as their lips parted he plunged a knife into her back. He believed that had he hesitated, for even a few seconds, she would have done the same to him.

He knew if his daughter were on a mission in Paris, she would face the same risks he had. The risks were always there.

It started to rain and he turned on his wipers. The spray from the tires of cars and trucks hung over the wet highway like a low fog.

A sign ahead: I-95, two miles.

Ray was in the right lane, and traffic started to bunch up. A semi was next to him in the left lane, and on this highway the exit ramp to I-95 was on the left. As the exit approached, he saw a space in front of the truck, flipped the turn signal, and floored the accelerator. The engine revved, the transmission downshifted, and the exhaust roared, as he overtook the semi and veered into the left lane just in time to make it onto the exit ramp.

Suddenly, a sea of red brake lights flashed in front of him, as traffic backed up from the merge onto I-95. Ray slammed on the brakes and felt the uncomfortable vibration of the ABS system, as it kept him from skidding out of control on the wet pavement. The distance between him and the car ahead shrank rapidly, and Ray heard the thump of his luggage shifting in the cargo area.

With less than ten feet of air in front of him, the brake lights went off and the car sped off into the thinning traffic ahead. Ray's foot quickly moved back to the accelerator to keep up with the new pace of traffic.

His heart still racing, he wiped the beads of perspiration from his forehead with his hand. *That was too close.*

After merging with the now sparse traffic in the right lane, he remembered the bottle of Scotch in his duffel. A sniff told him it hadn't broken.

There were so few cars now that he wondered what had caused the sudden backup. He looked in all three mirrors, but the semi wasn't in sight. It didn't matter anymore. He was very tired.

The heavy rain had lessened. A short distance ahead was the Kingsland exit and a sign for The Rest Inn Motel. Its bright yellow letters glowed in the mist, and below it, a red vacancy sign flashed a neon invitation.

Chapter 4

The parking lot was nearly empty, and of the few cars there, none were parked near the entrance or near each other. Ray took notice, and thought it odd. It ran against the familiar order of things, but he couldn't attach any significance to it. He parked near the front entrance, turned off the motor, and sat. The rain had stopped, but the gloom surrounding him seemed thick. Even the reflection of the neon lights on the puddled asphalt could not break it.

What time is it anyway? His watch had stopped at five thirty-two. He knew it was much later now, but how much? He felt so tired.

When he left home, he planned to have a drink at the bar in the motel, and think about what he would say to Olivia the next day. Now he craved sleep more than anything. He needed to muster his energy just to get out of the car.

The woman at the registration desk greeted him with a big smile. Her name "Darlene" prominently pinned on above her ample left breast. Her full upper figure was balanced by shapely rounded hips wrapped in a short tight skirt, but he was too tired to notice that.

Darlene saw how tired Ray looked. She had seen many weary travelers coming off the highway, looking no better than road kill, and she gave them all the same warm greeting and the promise of a good start in the morning.

"Hi, darlin'. Bet you're glad to get out of that weather? Do you have a reservation? Never mind, doesn't matter tonight, got plenty of room."

She looked through the glass door toward his car, and seeing no one in the passenger seat, offered him a single room, and placed a registration form on the counter. She ran his credit card and handed him the room key.

"Number nineteen, just outside and to the left."

Darlene pointed to a doorway leading to an adjoining room. "We've got a bar right here if ya want a nightcap, but to tell you the truth, I think you should just get some sleep. We do breakfast in there too, from seven to ten, and I gotta tell ya, we got the best coffee this side of the Shenandoah Valley."

With a weak "Thank you," Ray picked up the key, walked outside, and remembered to turn left.

He entered the room, closed the door behind him, stumbled to the bed, and collapsed.

Chapter 5

Too tired to close the curtains the night before, Ray awoke to the glare of the morning sun shining on his face. His mouth tasted like battery acid, and he still wore the clothes from the day before. The only thing he remembered was Darlene saying something about coffee.

"Coffee," he said as he sat up on the side of the bed. The room key was still in his hand. He felt strange, but not too strange to remember his noon appointment with Olivia. The clock on the nightstand displayed 8:00 a.m. He had to get some coffee, freshen up, and hit the road before nine.

When he entered the lobby, Darlene greeted him with a big smile. "Good morning darlin'. Coffee is fresh and hot. Just have a seat and Tommy will get ya a mug."

"Thanks," Ray said, and walked into the bar that was now set up for breakfast. There were two men, each alone at a table, and a woman who had her back to Ray. As a spy he was trained to size up any room when he entered, to see if anything didn't look right. Old habits don't die.

Ray sat a table on the side of the room with no windows. A scruffy looking kid with light brown hair and the oval corporate nametag walked over from the other side of the room. He looked younger than Jennifer, Ray thought, and he remembered she was now in Paris.

"Good morning, Mr. Walker," Tommy said as he set the steaming mug down in front of Ray.

"How do you know my name?" Ray said, looking up at the young man.

"Enjoy your coffee," Tommy said.

Silently Ray watched Tommy return to the coffee maker. He poured a large quantity of sugar into his mug, and stirred. The aroma from the breakfast buffet was good, but Ray wasn't hungry.

Over the rim of his mug Ray saw Darlene walking toward him from the buffet table. Now, she was wearing a snug, light blue waitress uniform, nametag still prominently displayed.

"Maybe that coffee will perk ya up," she said. She regarded him more circumspectly than she did the night before. "Want to try some breakfast today?"

"No thanks."

She turned and walked away. Ray almost smiled as he watched the casual sway of her hips.

He cautiously took a long sip of the hot brew and tried to enjoy the feeling as it went down, taking the stale taste from his mouth with it.

"It's okay to look," a woman's voice said.

"Huh?"

As he turned to see who was speaking he noticed the woman who had her back to him was no longer there.

"I said it's okay to look, actually she wants you to," the young woman said.

And who are you?" Ray said curtly.

"Ray, look at me. I know you're tired, drink some more coffee and try to focus."

"What the f . . ." He censored himself. He looked up slowly, first seeing her long shapely legs, not her dark skirt, red sweater, and then a pretty young face framed in long black hair that cascaded down over her perky breasts. *Pretty enough*, he thought, but he wasn't interested. He shook his head to clear the thought. "Do I know you?"

"Yes, you do," she said.

"I don't think so. Besides I don't have time for games. I just want to finish my coffee and get on the road," Ray said dismissively to the young woman as he caught Darlene's eye and pointed to his mug.

The young woman sat in the chair across from Ray and leaned forward.

"Ray, look at me. Look at my face," she said with force.

"It's too early in the day for this, and besides, I'm married . . ." Ray stopped and looked directly at her.

Darlene replaced his empty mug with a full one without saying anything. Ray didn't bother with sugar, and took a long swallow before focusing on his tablemate again.

"That's right. Focus. Who do you see?" she insisted.

He was wide-awake now. "It's not possible . . ."

"Ray, keep your mind open. Who do you see?"

"You remind me of a girl I used to know, Abby, but that was years ago and besides she's been dead for over twenty years." He felt like he wanted to cry, but no tears came to his eyes. He and Abby were told that if they were to have careers as spies it was impossible for them to become romantically involved. Reluctantly, they agreed, putting patriotism ahead of desire.

"Yes, you look just like Abby," he would have said if his throat had let the words out.

She had his attention, and smiled. He saw the look of love in her eyes.

"It can't be," he mouthed the words, but no sound came out.

She reached over the table and placed her hand on his.

Her voice was soft. "Relax Ray, its okay. You've been through a lot. You're still in shock. Give yourself a minute. Think about where you are. Remember how tired you were last night, and how strange you felt this morning."

"Yes," he said.

"You're not hungry this morning. When was the last time you ate?"

"I don't know, yesterday? On the road somewhere, maybe." He couldn't remember.

"And when was the last time you had to pee?"

"Sometime yesterday, when I filled up with gas, I think," he answered, ignoring the strangeness of her question.

"Right, and after that, remember what else happened? You got back on the road, it started to rain, and the road was very wet. You raced a semi to the exit ramp and you had to hit the brakes. Then you heard a thud you thought was your luggage shifting. But that's not what happened, is it Ray?" She waited for what she said to sink in.

Ray just stared at his coffee mug. All eyes in the room were on him.

"No it isn't," he whispered.

He felt her hand tighten its grip on his.

"Your mind was so tightly focused on Jennifer, and Paris, and Olivia, you couldn't think of anything else. What *did* happen, Ray? Tell me what *really* happened."

Ray slumped in his chair, his face tensed. Abby watched him reconstruct the events in his mind.

"The semi . . . it was a car carrier," he said weakly.

"And what else about the semi?" she said, her voice stronger again.

She saw his expression change as he looked up at her.

"The semi couldn't stop. I heard the thud, and then louder sounds, crunching metal and then, everything was orange, fire all over, and," He paused. "That was it."

"What do you mean by *it*?" She needed to hear him say the words.

"I'm dead?" It came out as a question.

"That's right, and you know I died in Geneva in nineteen eighty-five, right?"

"Right," he said, looking around the room. "And that means everyone else here is dead, too?"

Darlene was watching, a sad, but relieved look in her eyes. She nodded when she heard him say the words. When he looked at Tommy the young man smiled weakly and nodded, as the other guests watched.

Ray didn't speak. He looked around the room and examined everything carefully. It all looked so real, just like things did the day before. He couldn't see any otherworldly quality about this place. Nothing divine or menacing.

"Good. You're starting to remember. But it wasn't yesterday. You arrived here fourteen days ago, and each morning you'd come in for a mug of black coffee, and left. Instead of getting into your car, you would go back to your room for just a little more sleep. The next morning you would start again. That's why Tommy knows your name. That's why I am here for you now."

"Then you are . . . Abby," he said, reaching over to put his hand on the side of her face. "You really are Abby. I am so—" She put her finger in front of his lips. "You don't have to speak. Just know that I'm here for you. We will have all the time we need together, later."

"Together?"

"Yes, my sweet Ray, together," she said, as though she read his thoughts.

Darlene and Tommy were concerned. You weren't accepting the fact that you're dead."

"Yes, I understand now. I'm dead, just like you." His voice was flat.

"Yes, and everyone else in the room."

"Everyone?"

"That's right," Abby said.

Ray noticed the others had gathered around them.

Darlene spoke first. "Cigarettes got me back in '03."

Then Tommy. "Spring break '69. Tequila and acid don't mix."

A man in a dark suit. "It sounds cliché, but I got caught by a jealous husband, *in flagrante delecto*, as they say, '49."

The man in the pilot's uniform spoke last. "Pentagon, 9/11."

Ray smiled at each of them.

"Thank you," Abby said, "I think he's with us now."

Ray looked at Abby. The others went back to what they had been doing.

"What is this place?" he asked.

"Well, for one thing it is a restaurant."

"Yes," Ray said. "I'm hungry."

"That's a good sign. Wait here, I'll get you something."

Darlene smiled as Abby passed her on her way to the buffet and said, "Good job, honey."

"Right on!" Tommy said from behind the bar.

Chapter 6

Abby brought a plate of bacon, eggs, and toast for Ray.
Darlene brought two fresh mugs of coffee to the table.

"I know you have a lot of questions," she said as he ate, "but don't think about them now. You have enough to process. We all know what you are going through. I promise, you will be told everything you need to know."

Ray finished eating and pushed the plate away as Abby drank the last of her coffee.

He leaned over the table. "You said I was here for fourteen days?"

"Yes." She didn't want to have this conversation now, but she knew Ray well enough to realize she couldn't avoid it completely.

"What happened to Jennifer, and Ashley, and Wendy?" He looked concerned.

"You don't get to know about that. None of us do."

"What do you mean? If you asked me about Louis or Maurice I would tell you what happened after you were killed."

"Really?" she said.

"Yes, after you were killed . . ." He stopped. "I, I can't remember." He was embarrassed at his lapse of memory.

"Ray, it's not your memory. You can't tell me because these are things I am not supposed to know. None of us can know what happened to our loved ones after we die."

"Why?" He was resisting.

"You know why? Because we are not part of that world anymore. We're here, and they are there, and that's it. We can only go forward. You can understand that can't you?"

"Yes, if you say so."

"For whatever its worth, I think you can take some comfort in the thought that you probably had a very nice funeral. Everyone was there. I think Olivia would have been there too, and there was probably a lot of crying. Afterward, Olivia would have gone back to Suffern and lit a candle for you." It was a strain, but Abby managed to get it all out. She didn't know that his coffin contained only a skull and partial rib cage, which was all that was left of Ray after the fiery wreck.

She believed her funeral would have been roughly the same — her husband, Louis, and son, Maurice, crying as her white coffin was lowered into the ground next to her mother on Long Island. She would never know that Charles, her boss and longtime friend, had arranged for her funeral in Paris, since she no longer had any living relatives in America. She did not know that her husband Louis had been buried beside her a few years after her death. Many years later, her son, Maurice, would join them, and eventually Jennifer. Much later, there would be others.

She was correct to believe that in the custom of the Culper Spy Ring, Olivia lit a candle for each of them, at their secret headquarters in Suffern, New York.

"Let's go to my room, and we can talk. It's at the end of the walkway, and it will be good to get outside for a while."

Ray agreed, and they walked through the lobby to the door leading to the parking lot. Ray held the door for Abby to exit as a young woman carrying a baby entered. Once outside, Ray froze in his tracks at the realization that the woman and baby were both dead.

Abby stepped in front of him and looked directly into his eyes. "Ray, stay with me. Remember what we talked about. Everyone you will see from now on has died, just like we have. Do you understand? Everyone," she said, with her voice raised.

"Of course, it's just . . . I'm still getting used to the idea, that's all."

"Let's walk for a while, enjoy the sunshine, and no talking, okay?"

He nodded. She smiled, and held his hand as they walked to her room at the end of the building.

Chapter 7

Abby locked the door and turned to Ray, giving him a sly seductive smile.

A long time ago Ray used to think about being alone with Abby. Now, in another life, those old feelings began to return. He thought he felt his blood pressure rise, but didn't know if that was actually possible.

"Uh, Abby, we're both married and the oath, remember?"

She maneuvered him so that his back was to the bed and pushed him down to a sitting position, leaned over and put her forehead against his.

"Remember the words 'til death do us part? I think this qualifies, don't you?" she said, pushing him onto his back, jumping astride him, and putting her hands on his shoulders.

"Abby what are you—"

"Remember the night we met at the diner? Remember what we said in the parking lot? We agreed to put our Culper Ring loyalties ahead of our personal desires, but before we left I said to you, 'In another life.' That was a promise. I didn't say it that way, but it was. And you repeated it. 'In another life,' you said, and that was a promise, too."

He remembered the night, and how sad they both had been with the decision they felt compelled to make. Now they were together, and free from all of the oaths and vows that had kept them apart. He had wished for this moment since the first time they met, and now felt something stirring deep inside, in a place he didn't know still existed. Without saying a word, he pulled her down and kissed her lips, gently at first, with the uncertainty of a first kiss, and then with the ardor of a much younger man.

Kissing and groping, they undressed each other, until they both lay naked on the bed, exploring, and tasting each other until she was ready to let the full measure of his passion enter her own, and together they became one.

In the fire of their love, a bright white light enveloped them like a cocoon, and in that light they began a lifetime together. They did everything they would have done in their other lives. They married, and had careers, he as an accountant, and she as a teacher. But there was a difference now. Ray no longer had two lives. In this life he was not a spy. He was more focused on his family, and found greater satisfaction in his time with them.

The white light became yellow when they bought a small house, had children, and enjoyed raising a family together. Sometimes Abby would say they needed a larger house to contain all the love in their family, and that made Ray happier than he had ever known he could be.

The yellow light turned orange as their children went off to college, married, and had children of their own. For the first time, Ray and Abby shared the joy of being grandparents.

The orange light darkened, as Ray and Abby enjoyed retirement, while watching their grandchildren grow into young adults. They also got to travel and enjoy foreign destinations, this time without any secret meetings and codes.

As the orange light faded, they lay together having made love for the last time, and in each other's arms, their life together came to an end.

The light, which had enveloped them, disappeared, and they were once again in the motel room, naked and sweaty, tears of joy, and sadness, streaming from their eyes.

"It was more beautiful than I had ever imagined it could be," she said through faint sobs. "Was it that way for you, too?"

"Yes it was, and so much more. It seemed so real." Emotion choked his words.

"Ray, it *was* real. We *did* have a whole lifetime together, and in many ways this one was more real. We didn't have the distractions we had before. We could just enjoy each other and our families. No double lives this time."

"But, what about our children, Sam and Martha, and the grandkids?"

"They're just like in our other life. The kids and grandkids will have their own lives, but we don't get to see it. That's the way life is—any life, in any world." She didn't want to leave Ray, but she was being pulled to another place, and she growing impatient. She had dealt with these realizations years ago, and in a little while would do so again. It hurt her badly the first time, and later it might hurt worse, but she had no time for those feelings now.

"Ray, I do think of them, and love them, and know that they will live their lives without us, just like we did when our parents passed. You see?"

They lay there for a while in the afterglow of a lifetime, and Abby knew their time together was coming to an end — for real this time.

She turned to the clock on the nightstand. "Five thirty-two. We really have to go," she said softly.

"Wait! All of that happened in one day?" he said.

"Not exactly. We did have a real lifetime together, in another reality, but in this one it was just a day." She said it with hesitation, knowing the meaning was completely lost on him, at least for now.

Why can't we stay here forever?" he asked, hoping it could be possible.

"Because, my sweet, forever is a long time, and I have to move on now."

Ray's joy turned to sadness. The gift they received was more than he ever could have hoped for, in either life. In his gut he knew she was right, he felt a drawing too, but he had no way of interpreting this new feeling.

Abby got out of bed first, showered, and put on fresh clothes. Ray dressed in what he had been wearing, his luggage still in his car.

"Where are we going?" Ray asked.

"I have to check out now," she said.

"Why can't you stay in my room?" He was desperate.

"No, didn't you hear what I said? I have to move on now." The tugging was stronger, and there was urgency in her voice.

Ray locked the door behind them and followed Abby as she dragged her wheeled overnight case behind her with one hand and led him by the other.

"Checking out," Abby said to Darlene.

"You take care honey, thanks for coming," Darlene said cheerfully.

Abby turned to Ray and threw her arms around him one last time, and kissed him. "Ray, I love you, I always have, and I always will."

Before he could say anything she turned and walked out, suitcase in tow.

Darlene, called to him, "Mr. Walker, may I please have her room key?"

Ray looked at Darlene, quickly put the key on the counter, and turned to go after Abby. He pushed the doors open and rushed outside, but she was gone. He ran back in and shouted at Darlene, "Where did she go?"

"It was her time to move on," Darlene said softly, seeing the pain in his eyes.

"Move on to where?" Ray asked.

"I have no idea, but I would guess it's someplace we don't know anything about."

Gary Ader

Chapter 8

Having lost Abby for the second time, all Ray felt was anger. But it was unfocused. He had no idea who or what to be angry at.

He tried to remember everything that happened since Abby made him realize he had died. Each time he thought he had reasoned his way towards an understanding of his circumstances, he was confronted with something new, which further fueled his frustration over his inability to grasp at once the totality of his situation.

Even if he didn't want to admit it, he knew the accident he died in was his own fault. The Virginia State Police thought so, too. Their report stated the driver of the SUV was at fault for: "failure to yield the right of way, reckless driving, and failure to adjust to hazardous road conditions." Ray Walker would never know that.

He distracted himself from this train of thought by remembering that he and Abby did share a lifetime together. She said it was in another reality, and the thought confounded him. He wondered how many realities there were, and could it be possible for him to pass in and out of them as easily as he did with Abby. He planned to consider that more carefully later. Another realization: For the first time in his life he was completely alone. No friends or family. Now he was afraid *and* angry — confused by irreconcilable emotions.

He needed a drink. He sat at the far end of the bar, so he could see the room. An old habit. Tommy, in a white shirt and black bow tie, was now the bartender.

Ray ordered a double Scotch.

Tommy put a white paper napkin on the bar before setting the glass of scotch on it. The name of the motel, "THE REST INN," imprinted in bold red letters reminded Ray of another time and place. The drink was a lot more than a double. He looked up at Tommy.

"On the house, Mr. Walker," Tommy said. "I thought you could use a tall one."

"Thanks," Ray said, raising his glass to Tommy. "To new beginnings."

"To new beginnings," Tommy echoed.

Ray regarded him curiously. Tommy appeared to be about twenty years old, just as he was when he died in '69. In that case they were both about the same age. *Interesting* Tommy *gets to be a good-looking college kid for all eternity, and I will be old forever.* Who was better off? But then again, when he was with Abby he felt the way he had in college. Ray hoped the contents of the glass would put the brakes on these thoughts, and give his brain a timeout.

He took a swallow of the golden liquid, and let it go down slowly, enjoying the warm feeling inside. This was the first drink he had had since he arrived here, and the taste of Scotch greeted him like an old friend. *My only friend.*

Staring into the contents of his glass, he thought about Wendy, Jennifer, and Ashley. He wondered if they were well and happy, and then he thought about his other family, the one he had with Abby. That was weird. He took another drink.

He didn't feel his memories of them slipping away, but they were, and it would be one of the last times he would think about either family.

Now he was sad, angry, and afraid. Normally, anger would cancel out the other emotions, for a while anyway, but in Ray's current state, that was not the case. It was all becoming too much, and he took few deep breaths to fight off a panic attack. As he calmed down, an unfamiliar emotion joined the others — self pity — and it hurt. It was a luxury he had never allowed himself before. He didn't like it and wished for it to pass; it would, like healing from a serious operation, in imperceptible increments.

His ability to accept the idea that he was not in the same world he had been in, or thought he was in when he arrived at The Rest Inn, was strained. Nothing appeared different. If he had not been told that he had died and was now in some kind of afterlife, the thought would never have crossed his mind. Nothing he observed was in any way out of the ordinary, except for his lifetime in a day with Abby. He tried to rationalize it as a hallucination from a drug she put in his breakfast. The thought stuck. *She put it in my breakfast.* If she was really Abby, then everything else was real. If! It was the one variable he could not account for. He tried to picture a Venn diagram, but didn't know where to put Abby. She appeared to possess the ability to exist in more than one reality.

As he hoped, the alcohol took the edge off his emotional state, and his body began to feel more relaxed. Ray hoped this was only a very vivid dream, one from which he would soon awaken, probably with a hangover. But he never really believed that.

The thought disappeared when the thin man in a dark suit, the one who had been shot by a jealous husband, approached him.

"Mr. Walker, we weren't properly introduced earlier. My name is Spade, Donald Spade, and we do need to have a chat."

"Well, Donald, call me Ray, and what do you think we need to chat about?" Ray was as interested in chatting with Donald Spade right now as he was in having a root canal.

"There is some necessary business I must discuss with you. Will you join me at a table so we can have some privacy?" Seeing Ray's reluctance he added, "Please."

"Why? Do you think I want to hear the rest of your story?" Ray said. He was annoyed at the interruption, and hoped Donald Spade would get the hint.

"I think not," Spade said sternly. "But we do need to talk. Tommy, would you please bring my usual to the table?"

"Sure thing, Mr. Spade."

Ray followed Donald to the table, glass and napkin in hand. As they approached the table, he quickly maneuvered himself to take the seat facing the door, forcing his companion to sit with his back to the room.

Neither one of them took notice of the rumble of the motorcycle pulling up in front of the building.

"You really *can* give up that habit now," Spade said, annoyed. "You are not a spy anymore."

Ray was taken by surprise. "Who said I was a spy?"

Donald Spade sat straight-backed, hands folded on the table in front of him.

"Please, Mr. Walker . . . Ray . . . I have no time for games."

They were startled by a gruff male voice shouting, "Where's my girl? Where's my Linda Jean?"

"I don't know," they heard Darlene yell, running from the lobby to the bar, a man in a motorcycle jacket in pursuit, knocking over tables and chairs, making a straight line for Darlene.

"Where is she? What did you do with her?"

Ray tried to get up, but Donald reached across the table and held his arm with an iron grip.

"Biker Dude" caught up to Darlene, grabbed her by the arms, and pushed her against the wall so hard the bottles on the shelves rattled.

His sweaty face and dirty beard were inches from her. "Tell me where she is, you fucking whore, or I'll break you!" he roared. Darlene grimaced at the spit flying in her face with each word.

"Lawrence! Juan!" Tommy yelled.

Immediately, two large men emerged from a back room, and Ray settled back into his seat to watch.

Lawrence, tall, muscular, and black, yanked Biker Dude off Darlene, and threw him to the floor, face down. Juan, who carried a lot more weight, was faster than he looked, and jumped on top of him, twisting his tattoo-covered arms behind his back.

"You okay, Darlene?" Lawrence asked.

"Yeah, I'll be fine. Just a little shaken, that's all."

The Biker Dude was still screaming obscenities when Juan lifted him off the floor by his arms, which were still twisted behind his back.

Lawrence got right up in his face, and calmly tried to talk him down. "It's okay man. Quiet down. Your girlfriend is okay. Take it easy, and I'll explain everything."

He really tried, but Biker Dude kept struggling and cursing. Lawrence nodded. Juan pulled his arms back tighter, and Biker Dude tried to kick Lawrence in the groin with one of his steel-tipped boots.

"Sorry, man," Lawrence said, as he dodged the kick, before leaning in with a solid right to the jaw.

Juan let go, and Biker Dude went down like a sack of potatoes.

Lawrence bent over to check him out. "Nothing broken," he announced. "He'll be out for a while. Take him to room thirteen."

"Thanks guys," Darlene said, as Lawrence and Juan took either end of Biker Dude, and carried him out.

"Sorry for the inconvenience folks. Shows over," she said, and started righting overturned tables and chairs.

Tommy silently put a martini on the table in front of Donald.

"Thank you, Tommy, and I think you had better get one for Darlene."

"Yes sir." Tommy said, making a beeline for the bar.

"What's that about room thirteen?" Ray asked.

"It's a place where he can cool down and not be a threat to anyone. People with a violent nature become aggressive when faced with new circumstances," Donald said calmly.

"And are Lawrence and Juan going to teach him a lesson about how to treat a lady?" Ray asked.

"Certainly not. They're not thugs. It is as I said, he needs some time in private to adjust, and Lawrence and Juan will explain things to him when he wakes up."

"But what happened to his girlfriend? Ray asked.

Donald explained with an omniscient knowledge, *or a convincing guess.* Ray wasn't sure which. "Sometimes, people who die together in traumatic situations arrive here together. If for some reason one of them doesn't belong here, they must be redirected to their correct destination."

Ray had no idea what Donald was talking about, and chose not to ask. He already had too much information to process, and no idea how much more was yet to come.

He watched Donald take a long satisfying drink of his martini.

"I think we are on equal footing now," Donald said. Let us get down to business. Ray, I am an attorney, and as such, I must give you, if you will forgive the expression, a crash course in how things work here."

"Ouch," Ray said, choosing to gaze around the room as he spoke. "So here I am, dead in a bar with a lot of other dead people, and I wind up with a divorce lawyer who can't keep his pecker in his pants, who wants to give me a tour of the afterlife." Ray finished his tirade staring directly into Donald's eyes.

"I'll credit that little outburst to the alcohol, and your state of disorientation, but nevertheless, that is roughly correct," Donald said, as he peered down his long thin nose at Ray.

"Who says you must?" Ray demanded to know.

"That is part of what I want to explain. You do need to relax and open your mind. I know that is not an easy thing for you to do, but it is necessary. Will you listen with an open mind?" Donald emphasized each word of the question.

Ray contemplated his situation. He knew he had little choice. He had to learn about this world, to try to understand it as best he could, in order to survive. Maybe survive wasn't the right word; function would be more accurate. He needed to be able to function in this world. He nodded his assent.

"That is part of it," Donald started again. "There are certain things one just seems to know here. It will happen to you as well. In fact, it already did. I never told you I was a divorce lawyer, and you never told me you were a spy. One just gets a feeling about things. You don't know how or why, but you do. Sometimes it is a feeling of something you must do, in other cases something you must not do, and it is always best to follow those feelings."

Ray thought Donald would call his knowledge about the Biker Dude and his girlfriend just one of those feeling.

"Okay, I'll take that at face value for now. But where are we?" Ray demanded.

"This place, or more precisely, this *world*, is called The Dim*edium*. We call it *The Dim*. To anticipate your next question, it is neither heaven nor hell, it is just *The Dim*." Donald took another sip of his martini. "If it helps, you can think of this as an alternate reality. It is where you are now, but not necessarily where you will always be. At some point in time you will probably move on, just as Abby did."

"Move on to where?" Ray asked.

"It is something we do not know, only that most people eventually do move on, and I suspect they do not all go to the same place. People come here for a reason. In fiction, they say, "to take care of unfinished business." Perhaps so, but we only know that at some point they do move on, to let us call it, the next level, and I cannot discuss any of that with you." Donald's tone preempted any challenge from Ray.

Were it not for the dulling effects of the alcohol, Ray thought his head would have exploded. "Is God running things here?"

"An inevitable question, and the precise answer is 'no.' In this world you will not find one church or house of worship of any denomination. The notion of religion does not exist in this reality. Frankly, I found it troublesome at first, since I was brought up in a rather strict religious home, but over time I have found the experience . . . liberating." Donald raised his eyebrows.

"Everything here looks just like where I came from," Ray said. "What happened to the churches?"

"Those places are parks, coffee shops, many things," Donald said with a shrug. "You don't notice their absence."

"Coffee shops? Do they have Starbucks here?" Ray had to ask.

Donald laughed, the first and only time he would do so in Ray's presence.

"Actually, they do."

"Hmmm," Ray continued, "so there *is* a God."

"Ray, you must take this more seriously."

"From where I'm sitting that's asking a lot," Ray said. "But, if you want serious, how's this. First, do either God or the Devil really exist in any reality?" Ray thought rewording the question would elicit a different response. "Second, are good and evil still dueling it out in this world . . . *The Dim*?"

Donald regarded Ray for a moment. "Well . . . to put it in terms you can understand, there is no God, as you think of it, which of course, obviates the existence of the devil. That in no way precludes the existence of a higher power. That said, good and evil—or let's say, bad—are merely the result of the choices we make. Free will exists in all worlds. Striving for good is always a noble quest, and you should think of goodness as a rare gem with many facets, reflecting light in different directions. What you see depends on what angle you view it from."

Ray didn't say anything. He absorbed Donald's words at about the same rate as he did the alcohol from his drink.

"More to the point, knowledge is the good you will be seeking in *The Dim*. Think of it as a quest. The specifics of your quest will manifest themselves to you as you make your journey. It will be critical for you to maintain an open mind, and to accept things as you find them. Your travels and experiences in the other world have been varied, and I might add, far more extensive than those of most individuals. As a result, you believe yourself to possess a great deal of knowledge about a great many subjects. Nevertheless, there is a lot you have yet to learn."

Ray considered the veracity of Donald's words as he finished his drink. Yes, he did know many things, and he had the self-awareness to realize there were many aspects to life and the human condition he had never taken the time to contemplate. His life, or *lives,* as he thought of them now, had kept him in a perpetual struggle to maintain equilibrium. In his secret life as a spy, he had faced unforeseen dangers and committed acts he never thought himself capable of. His public life was that of a family man and businessman. Keeping those two lives discrete, and seamlessly transitioning between them rarely allowed time to reflect on the bigger picture.

"I suppose that's true," Ray finally conceded.

"Knowledge lies at the nexus of two elements, experience, and observation," Donald continued. "Objective contemplation of knowledge will enable you to transcend to the next level. That is wisdom. It is what you must seek here in *The Dim.* Beyond wisdom is enlightenment, an awakening. It is something you must strive for, but frankly, unless your attitude changes, it is unlikely you will ever achieve that state of being."

Screw you! Ray thought.

"Nevertheless, it is of the utmost importance that you keep your mind open to new ideas and all possibilities, especially those which you never accepted before. Centuries ago, in the other world, enlightenment promoted science and reason over myth and superstition. As long as it did not contradict another superstition: religion. I suppose it was a necessary step in the evolutionary process. Here, in *The Dim*, enlightenment is the acceptance of the existence of that which science and reason could not explain in the other world. In *this* world, the stuff of myth and legend are a part of science, and in the absence of religious doctrine, are able to exist freely. Myths and legends all have some basis in fact. Human history is rife with examples, and all of them are worthy of contemplation. Accepting these things as part of this world is an essential part of your quest."

Ray held up his glass, signaling for Tommy to bring him a refill.

Some part of what Donald said did ring true. He realized it was the one aspect of himself in which he was deficient. Yes, he had seen and done many things. He knew how things worked, and how to navigate through many of life's perils, but his focus was always on his immediate situation. He never took the trouble to see the bigger picture, or to contemplate what others saw and felt. His worldview was limited by what he needed to accomplish. His survival often depended upon that. Now, Donald told him he needed to broaden his view and train himself to perceive the many levels of existence in what was broadly called the human condition.

"Anyway," Donald continued, "it was late when you and Abby came back to the lobby, so Darlene agreed to let you stay another night. But you must leave here tomorrow morning. You can have breakfast first, but you *must* check out by eleven," Donald said flatly.

"Leave for *where? Home?*" Ray asked.

"Absolutely not. You have no home in this world," Donald said sternly.

"Then where the hell am I supposed to go?" Ray was running o out of patience.

"That cuts to the point of it, and by the way we do *not* use that word here. Nevertheless, you can go anywhere you want, but not home. If you try to go there, or to any other place to which you had a strong emotional attachment, you will find yourself regretting it."

Ray mind was racing, trying to find loopholes in this warning.

"I mean that in the strongest sense of the word," Donald said. "Do not even consider hovering on the fringes of those places. I suspect that at some point you will want to test this for yourself, like a child seeing how close to the flame he can put his hand before getting burned. In your case, it will be far more painful. I am telling you this with the greatest hope that you will choose to avoid this experience."

"What if I need to pass by one of them to get to where I'm going?"

"This is not a negotiation. It is a warning. Do not go to those places. In addition, people you were close to in the other world do not exist in this one, even those who have predeceased you. Abby was a special case, and she no longer exists in *The Dim*. In fact, it is unlikely, but not impossible that you will meet any of the people you had known. In your case that may be a plus," Donald said.

"And what does that mean?" Ray challenged.

"I think you know the answer, but if you insist on hearing it, I am referring to the young woman in Paris for example, or her father, with whom you had an encounter in Hong Kong. Is that enough?"

"I get it." Ray said, not wanting to be reminded.

Donald sat silently watching Ray recall those events in excruciating detail.

"Again, so where am I supposed to go?" Ray demanded.

"Anywhere you want. You have your vehicle, and you will always have enough money for the things you need: gas, lodging, food, and such. Don't plan on buying a yacht or real estate though," Donald said.

"So I just travel and what?"

"*That* is up to you. You will find things in *The Dim* generally work the way they did in the other world, with some exceptions that you will notice in due course."

"*That's* a big help," Ray said. "What about computers and the internet?"

"Your laptop will work here, and the Internet does exist, although you will not have any need of either. But if you choose to avail yourself of them, there are some websites that will be unavailable to you. I know you will want to try, but it will be futile."

"Are these rules for everyone or just me?" Ray asked.

"I understand why this is all so difficult for you. You are resisting, like you did for the first fourteen days you were here. *The Dim* is where you are now. You must follow its ways, and go with the flow, so to speak," Donald said, trying to bring his encounter with Ray to a conclusion, without answering his last question.

"Anything else?" Ray asked, hoping there wasn't.

"Yes, there are certain rules of etiquette you should observe here."

"Seriously?" Ray asked incredulously.

"Yes, seriously," Donald continued. "It is impolite to ask anyone how, when, or where they died in the other world. If they wish you to know, they will tell you, otherwise never ask. You will also find it advisable not to disclose the circumstances of your own demise with anyone you do not come to know well, and even then . . ." Donald shrugged as his voice trailed off.

"Is that it?" Ray said, hoping Donald would notice his irritation.

"No, there is one more thing. Do take a shower and change your clothes. People in *The Dim* do have a sense of smell."

"Will you be moving on?" Ray asked.

"That's another question you should not ask. But no, I will be remaining here for a time," Donald said, as he got out of his chair. Having done his job, he wanted to put an end to this conversation.

Ray stood, and Donald extended his hand. "With the right attitude," he said, "you should find satisfaction in your quest. Good luck, and be careful out there." Donald shook his hand once, turned, and left.

Ray wondered what he meant about being careful. He was dead. What else could happen? And, what did *luck* have to do with anything, except for the randomness of his choice of direction when he left The Rest Inn?

Gary Ader

Chapter 9

In the morning, Ray, now showered and in clean clothes, opted for breakfast and coffee before checking out. The woman with the baby sat at one of the tables eating and breastfeeding.

How does that work here? They're both dead, and she has to raise a kid here, and the baby grows up and . . . No, Tommy never got older. Will the baby stay a baby as long as they are in The Dim*?*

More unanswered questions.

Ray saw other guests in the bar/breakfast room. A teenage girl dressed in black, with tattoos and piercings, sat alone at a table, looking around the room. Long sleeves concealed the answer to the question he wondered about. An elderly couple, she with a walker, he with a cane, both smiled serenely, as he helped her transition to a chair. A fireman still in his fire suit searched the room, floor to ceiling, for a nonexistent fire.

"No fire here," Lawrence said. "You can relax now buddy, take off your equipment, and have some coffee and breakfast."

With a look of bewilderment, the fireman complied, and Lawrence brought him a plate piled high with food from the buffet.

Ray wondered what quests Donald would task them with. Would they also be seeking wisdom, or something else? Would he encounter any of them on his own quest?

His train of thought was interrupted when five elementary school children were ushered in by a young man, presumably their teacher. The children's dry-eyed expressions were of shock and horror. *Shit!* Ray turned away not wanting to think of the madness that sent them to *The Dim*.

Biker Dude was at a table toward the back of the room. Ray remembered Lawrence hitting him once on the jaw, but now there was also a cut on his nose and a blackened eye. Juan sat with him, and they talked quietly.

Biker Dude had a rough night. Lawrence had tried two more times to calm him down. When he woke up this morning, he was no longer the wild ball of anger he was the night before. Juan was sitting in a chair next to the bed.

"*Buenos dias, amigo*, time to start a new day," Juan said.

Biker Dude touched his aching face, wincing as he found the sources of his pain. He slowly opened his eyes, one a little less than the other, and saw Juan. "Don't hit me, man. I'm cool now," he said, raising his arms in front of his face.

"I know man. You're okay. It's just you and me," Juan said. "Lawrence isn't here."

Biker Dude sat up on the bed. Each man recognized the tattoos on the others arms and necks. Jailhouse tats. They had more in common than Ray would ever know. It was a bond that had given Juan the opportunity he needed to help Biker Dude accept the new realities of his existence, which made no allowance for the reflexive violence he had demonstrated the night before. Juan brought breakfast and coffee to the table. Afterward,

Biker Dude would get his orientation to *The Dim* from Juan.

When Juan looked toward Darlene, she took the coffee pot and moved cautiously to their table and refilled their cups. Without prompting, Biker Dude gave Darlene an emotional apology for hurting her with his hands and his words. The tears in his eyes begged her for forgiveness. She said she forgave him, and patted him on the shoulder before returning to the coffee station to get a fresh cup for Ray, who had just walked in.

Donald, still in his black suit walked over to them, placing one hand on each man's shoulder and spoke to them, like a referee before a boxing match, only today there would be no fighting. He walked away leaving the two men to their quiet conversation.

The diversity of guests at The Rest Inn was not lost on Ray, who took in everything he saw, knowing he would have to put all of the pieces together. When he finished his coffee, he went to the front desk, where Darlene was now standing.

"How are you doing?" Ray asked, noticing the bruises on her arms.

"I'm okay, really. He didn't mean it. He was just scared and confused. It happens once in a while."

"I guess every job has its rough spots," Ray said, putting his room key on the counter. "Thanks for the hospitality, and you can keep bragging about the coffee. Oh, I didn't see Tommy. Please tell him I said thanks for the drink."

"I would if I could, but he moved on this morning. I'm sure gonna miss that kid. Anyway, which way are you heading?" Darlene asked.

"Any way, I guess, it doesn't matter."

"Well, for whatever it's worth, I always think of that song, ya know the one about changes in latitude?"

"That's a good idea. Maybe a visit to Key West would be a good start." Ray smiled at the prospect of embarking on a new adventure.

Darlene came around the counter and surprised him with a big hug and a kiss on the cheek. Ray held on as long as he could, enjoying the feel of her curves against his body. When she leaned back he gave her a gentle lingering kiss on the lips.

"What's that for?" she said softly, as she opened her eyes.

"Being you," Ray said, wishing he could spend more time with her. "I'll stop in when I pass this way again," he added, not realizing that less than twenty-four hours before he had stood on the same spot and said a final goodbye to Abby.

Darlene smiled.

Chapter 10

Ray started his SUV for the first time since his arrival.
All instruments read normal, his gas tank was full, and
his satellite radio preset channels still played his favorite
music. His cell phone was in the console, the battery
was charged, and he had a signal, but nobody to call.

Darlene stood outside the front door of The Rest Inn,
and waved as Ray drove out of the parking lot. She
watched as he stopped at the traffic light at the entrance
ramp before turning on to I-95 southbound. She too,
wished they could have had more time together. He
was different than most of the other men she had met
here.

She didn't see Donald standing behind the glass
doors watching her wave goodbye to Ray Walker, who
was now officially a citizen of *The Dim*.

When Ray looked in his rearview mirror, all he saw
were the Old Dominion Lanes and a large parking lot.
The Rest Inn and Darlene no longer existed for him.
That realization gave him a chill.

The light changed, and he made a left turn onto the
entrance ramp, cautiously merging into the flow of
traffic. He set his cruise control at a notch above the
posted speed limit and stayed in the center lane, leaving
the left lane to the speeders and the right lane to the
overly cautious.

There was no looking back, and that was more than
a metaphor. He had to stay in the moment. He had a lot
of information to sort out. In fact, everything he could
remember since his arrival in *The Dim* was in need of

analysis. He made a conscious effort to put those thoughts on hold, and to stay focused on his immediate surroundings, now moving past him at seventy-five miles an hour.

Ray knew it was about noon, and with the sun directly above in a cloudless sky, the day didn't seem as bright as he thought it should.

He looked at other cars and recognized the makes and models, but their colors seemed off. Other drivers, men and women, young and old, all looked nondescript, and none looked in his direction as he changed lanes to get around slower traffic. The presence of trucks and RVs lent a sense of normalcy to the surroundings, but it still didn't seem real. Road signs announced upcoming exits using the incentives of food, fuel, and lodging to lure motorists off the highway. Billboard pollution was just as annoying as it always had been, but many of the products were unfamiliar.

It was less than a hundred miles from Richmond to the state line, but two hours and a hundred and fifty miles later Ray had not reached it. He stopped for gas, and his credit card worked at the pump. Inside he selected a snack and went to the counter to pay for it. He hadn't checked before, but the money he had when he left home was still there.

"Good afternoon," Ray said.

"Afternoon," the short heavyset woman behind the counter said without a smile.

"What day is today?"

She just stared at him.

"I said, what day is—"

"I heard ya," she said. "Just figurin' you must be new here."

"Yes, I guess I am, and I'm still trying to get used to things here in the . . . here," he said.

"Well, today is Tuesday," she said.

"And the date?"

"You're just full of questions, ain't ya? Well, as far as you're concerned today is October twenty-sixth," she said, seeing he wanted her to finish. "And don't go askin' me the year. It don't matter none. Unless you're fixin' to buy somethin' else, I suggest you get back on the road. I'm guessin' you got a lot of miles to cover and not much daylight to do it in."

So much for southern hospitality.

Ray left not knowing what she meant about the daylight, since it was only two o'clock. He struggled to remember. The day he left home (the last day of his former life) was October 25th. So all of the time he spent at The Rest Inn only equated to one day, *Dim* time, or was is it Ray Walker time?

He wasn't on the road long before billboards for "South of the Border" began appearing. That's when he noticed a semi moving up fast from behind, the driver flashing his headlights for Ray to either speed up or move over. Ray chose the latter. He didn't feel comfortable moving back into the center lane until the truck was well ahead of him.

Knowing it should be about twelve hundred miles from Richmond to Key West, he thought he would break his trip just south of Jacksonville, about half way. At the speed he was traveling, and allowing for rest stops he should arrive in Jacksonville about eight, add another half hour to get past the city, and find a place to rest for the night.

By five o'clock it was dark.

By eight o'clock he had traveled just over seven hundred miles, and was still, according to the road signs, well over a hundred miles from Jacksonville. It didn't make sense. He had traveled this road dozens of times over the years and knew the distances between every rest stop. He had no way to account for the variation. The only thing he could do was to continue until he needed to rest. The next exit off the highway led to Hilton Head Island, South Carolina, where he knew there would be a choice of motels and cheap restaurants.

A sign for the Sea-Ray Inn sat on a pylon above the motel.

Ray took it as a sigil, and turned into the parking lot of the one-story motel. He sat staring at the entrance. Nothing looked unusual. He was hungry and had to pee, so he figured this was nothing like his arrival at The Rest Inn.

A thin, bald man wearing a faded "I heart Hilton Head" tee shirt checked him in and gave him the key to Room 19, turned away and barely managed a "Have a good night," before disappearing behind a curtain.

Ray brought what he needed for the night from his luggage into the room, leaving the big suitcase in his car. He took a legal pad and pen from his overnight bag and walked over to the Carolina-Dina, just down the road. It wasn't far, only a gas station separating it from the motel.

He was hungry, but not jonesing for anything in particular, so he ordered a burger, fries, and a coke. It wasn't the healthiest choice, but did it really matter in *The Dim?*

While waiting for his dinner, Ray decided to try and sort out exactly what he knew to be true in his new world. He started to make notes on a legal pad. First, he had to decide if there was evidence to suggest that he was, in fact, dead. He could be in a coma, or experiencing a drug-induced hallucination, or maybe he had had a stroke. Insanity was also up for consideration.

Fact: After he cut off the semi to get to the exit ramp to I-95, and had to hit the brakes, he never saw the semi again, nor any of the other traffic he tried to avoid.

Fact: He didn't take drugs and was probably in too good health to have had a stroke . . . probably. Insanity was the only thing he could not rule out, but he believed he knew himself well enough to be able to tell he was sane. But wasn't that what they all said in the psych ward?

Conclusion: The accident and his death in the other world were probably real.

Fact: Abby said he had been in *The Dim* for two weeks before she made him accept the fact he had died.

Fact: He spent what he perceived as a lifetime with Abby in what was apparently a single day. Then he spent one more night at the Rest Inn. Fifteen days.

Fact: The surly clerk at the fuel stop told him today's date was the day after the date he left home.

Fact: Of all the gas stations between here and Richmond, nobody could have known where he would stop. If he believed that the whole world was in on the plot to deceive him, then he would be paranoid. He didn't, ergo he wasn't.

Conclusion: He had in fact died, and now existed in another reality, one similar to, but not identical to, the one he had known. Also, distance and time were not constants in *The Dim*. (He vowed to reconsider after gaining more information.)

Ray looked up when the waiter, a chubby kid with scruffy black hair, put his food and drink on the table.

"Writing a novel?" the young man asked.

"No, just making some notes, thanks," Ray said, dismissively. He didn't intend to be rude; he just wanted to keep his train of thought.

He took a bite of his burger and washed it down with some Coke, and noticed the television on the wall. Dale Earnheart was leading the Old Dominion 500. Yup, he thought, this is NASCAR country. He tried the fries.

"Wait!" a voice in his head screamed.

Ray got up and went over to the counter. The chef, a burly man wearing a paper hat, had his back to Ray and was watching the TV.

"Excuse me, is that a rerun on the TV?" Ray asked.

"Are you kiddin'? That's live. Ol' number three is going to win in two more laps," the chef said, pointing to the blue number tattooed on his forearm.

Ray returned to his seat. He knew that in the other world, Dale Earnhardt Sr. had died in a spectacular crash at the Daytona Speedway in 2001, but here in *The Dim,* he was still tearing up the track. Enough for tonight. Ray didn't bother finishing his dinner, or waiting for a check. He left a twenty-dollar bill on the table and walked out.

The gas station was closed, and the combination of a light cloud cover and the lights from the diner and motel obscured his view of the night sky.

He was tired, but his mind was still racing ahead of sleep. He thought about the notes he had made, the facts he knew, and the conclusions he had drawn. But he was wrong. His logic had stopped short of the truth.

He now reasoned that in the other world he had died. Everyone here died in the other world. Abby told him that. But here, in *The Dim*, he and everyone else were very much alive. He needed to eat, pee, and then eventually he would sleep. He had a sense of agency, was able to perceive his surroundings and interact with others, and knew that eventually he would have to satisfy other human needs as well.

Ding!

The tiniest of bells sounded in his head, just once. Ray had never heard it before, but knew what it was. He had transcended knowledge, and achieved a minuscule bit of wisdom. To his own surprise, his first thought was that Donald would be pleased if he knew. Or did he *already* know?

Before sleep overtook him, Ray made a mental note to skip the Coke and fries next time.

Gary Ader

Chapter 11

The sun was halfway to its zenith when Ray opened one eye enough to look at the bedside clock. Barely awake, he showered with his eyes closed. He knew where everything was, including the soap. It wasn't until he went to the sink to shave that he noticed. He looked younger—not a kid of twenty like Tommy, but more like a man of forty. His hair was full and mostly black, only a little grey at the temples. He backed away from the mirror and noticed his physique was leaner and his muscles more defined.

Then he watched the color drain from his face as he realized that he was forty when he went to Paris. He was forty when he killed Natalie Dufré, only seconds before she would have killed him. He had to put the thought out of his mind. After all, it was quite literally in another lifetime.

He wondered if the change was supposed to remind him of Paris, or had something to do with his quest. Would it be better if people didn't see him as on old man? He decided to accept the gift without further question.

At the Carolina-Dina, the waiter who served him the night before greeted him with a casual familiarity, which made Ray think his appearance had changed the day before, and he hadn't noticed.

With a full stomach, and a tank full of gas, Ray got back on the highway. He tried to calculate how far he could travel today, considering his shortfall the day before. He hoped to make it to Ft. Lauderdale.

Again, it was dark by five in the afternoon. By seven-thirty he had reached Daytona Beach, and decided to stop for the night. The Winner's Circle Motel was a step up from the night before and had a restaurant and bar combo like The Rest Inn. This time, Room 19 was much more comfortable.

Ray enjoyed a beer with dinner and watched NASCAR races on the screen above the bar. He noticed a number of single women watching the TV. He fantasized about them for a while, but decided this was not the time. He had to get an early start to make it to Key West the next day.

The bar had been reconfigured as a breakfast buffet in the morning, just like at The Rest Inn. By eight o'clock he was on the road, heading south, a fresh cup of coffee in the cup holder.

By one o'clock, a green sign announced he was entering Palm Beach County. After sixty-five miles, the next sign he saw was Ft. Lauderdale. As he traveled further south, the weather had become more tropical. In the midday heat he could see the humidity hanging in the air over the highway.

By three o'clock, he had passed Miami. "Key West — 125 miles," the sign read. The maximum speed limit was fifty, but slowed to thirty-five through Islamorada and Marathon. In another two and a half hours he should be there.

The atmosphere of the Keys had an effect on him. He began to relax and enjoy the scenery *and* the ocean. It was a nice change after two days of interstate driving. He hadn't decided how long he would stay in Key West, but he did plan to relax, drink, and enjoy whatever pleasures he might find. He wondered if he might meet *The Dim* version of Papa Hemmingway at Sloppy Joe's. The thought made him smile.

By five-thirty, as he traveled southwest, the sun was still above the top of the windshield as Ray crossed the bridge to Key West, roughly two hours earlier than he thought he would.

He checked into the Mile Zero Motel, a small beachfront inn, and was given the keys to Room 19— *again*. No longer surprised at the coincidence, he wondered if Donald was doing this just to mess with his head. It didn't matter. The room was large and comfortable. Sliding doors opened onto a small patio with a table and chair, and a view of the beach. The perfect place for doing nothing.

By the time he settled in, the sun was sinking below the horizon. Ray saw a green flash as he stepped outside.

Looking down the street ahead of him, he could see the ceiling fans slowly rotating inside Joe's bar.

Gary Ader

Chapter 12

The evening breeze brushed Ray's face with the warm salty air that was part of the magic of Key West.

For the first time since Ray arrived in *The Dim,* he felt relaxed. More than fifteen hundred miles of highway separated him from The Rest Inn—and Donald. Even though he had visited the Keys before, he felt detached from them, and that was good. As of now, they had zero emotional content for him, and he felt safe.

In *The Dim,* Sloppy Joe's was just "Joe's," and seemed busy for a Tuesday night. Ray sat at the end of the bar with a good view of the three-man band. Although Joe's had a reputation for the best bar food in the Keys, Ray had already decided on a liquid dinner.

"What'll it be?" the woman behind the bar asked.

"Scotch . . . no make it a beer tonight," Ray said. He usually would have ordered Scotch, but decided he could sit at the bar longer if he had a few beers.

"Just get here?" the waitress asked, putting a Pilsner glass on a paper napkin with Joe's stamped on it in bold red letters.

"Which *here,* the Keys or *here*-here?" he said looking at the napkin.

"Either. Both." She was curious about this stranger.

"First night in the Keys," Ray said. "A couple of weeks here, or so they tell me. Why?"

"Just wondering. It's just that you look like you belong here," she said.

Ray looked surprised. He knew that the Keys had been a mecca for LGBT people years before they added the Q.

"No, I didn't mean *that*," she said. "I can tell you're as straight as they come."

"Well, I *am* straight, but not narrow," Ray said.

"That's what I mean," she laughed. "You're not uptight. A lot of the newbies I see here seem lost, or act like they're looking for something, but you don't. You're just like, takin' it all in, aren't ya?"

"Yeah, I guess you could say that." *She can, but I can't. I'm supposed to be looking for knowledge and wisdom.*

Ray had been noticing the other patrons. Single men or women gazing blankly at the band, or into space. Couples together, looked detached from each other, as if trying to find shelter from loneliness, or so he imagined.

Sitting at a table at the end of the bar, farthest from the band, four men were engaged in quiet conversation. They looked more like conspirators than guys enjoying a night out. In the opposite corner of the room, at another table, were five women leaning in as if exchanging confidences.

"Well, you picked a good night to show up," said the barmaid. "This band is a hell of a lot better than the last one. You wouldn't believe it, but we do get tired of listening to Jimmy Buffet music after a while . . . *but . . .* most of the tourists expect it."

"Tourists in *The Dim*?" Ray asked, without thinking.

"You know what I mean, people that don't plan on stayin' here—like you."

Ray saw the irony, smiled at her, and, for the first time, took notice of her features. A deep tan made it hard to tell her age, somewhere between thirty and forty, he guessed. A shaggy mane of straw blonde hair brightened her appearance. And she had a beautiful smile. To Ray, almost any woman with a beautiful smile was a beautiful woman. *QED.*

"I'm Brenda, and I'm guessing you're going to be here a lot." She smiled, and extended her hand.

"Ray," he said, taking her hand and holding it. "I probably will."

"My days off are Sunday and Monday, so I'll be here for the next three nights, six till closing." She withdrew her hand. "Want a refill?"

He looked at her eyes and her smile for a long moment before answering, "Sure." As she walked to the other end of the bar, he noticed the way she moved. Her long tan legs and lean body looked more like an eighteen-year-old. He wondered about the parts of Brenda that weren't tanned, and it felt good. In *The Dim* he was free to think about such things. But thoughts were one thing, actions another. Abby was one thing, but this was uncharted territory. Then again, he always liked visiting new destinations. Such were the thoughts filling his mind, each time Brenda filled his glass.

With each refill they talked. Ray told her about his trip from Richmond, and how the drive, the sky, the texture of *The Dim*, all seemed different. There were other things, too. Ambivalent feelings he could not yet express.

As a bartender Brenda was a professional listener, and she did listen to everything Ray said, without offering any information about herself, only about the bar and the island. After three days alone in the car he was glad to have someone to talk to, and always enjoyed female company. But Ray was a professional too, a spy in the other world, and he heeded Donald's advice, and his own instincts. He avoided any discussion of his former life, or questions about Brenda's.

It was almost one o'clock when Ray paid his tab in cash, leaving an extra twenty for Brenda, and walked back to the hotel under a clear dark sky.

Lying in bed, the alcohol still buzzing in his head, he thought about Brenda, and the four men at the table, and Brenda again. He wondered if they were connected. He heard the *ding* of a small bell in his head, and fell asleep.

Chapter 13

A screeching sound in a dream awakened Ray, but when he opened his eyes the sound continued. It was outside his room, and he went to the sliding doors. A seagull stood on the patio table. When Ray looked out, the bird gave one last squawk and flew away. It was nature's wakeup call. He glanced at the clock and saw the digital numerals change from 9:00 a.m. to 9:01 a.m. He dressed and went out for breakfast.

A block past Joe's bar was the Oceanside Diner. Ray slid into a booth and when the server approached, he ordered coffee, eggs, toast, and bacon. No need to look at a menu. Before his morning coffee he had no desire to discuss specials or menu options. He could order the same breakfast in any diner in the country, and it would come out the same, more or less, and that was fine.

"Your order will be right out," the waitress said, as she refilled his cup.

As she walked away a man slid into the same booth opposite Ray.

"Who the hell are you?" Ray said.

"Ray, I'm a friend of Brenda's."

"And?"

"Okay, so you're not a morning person, I get it, but just listen. My name is Tony. I was one of the guys at the corner table in Joe's last night."

Tony's accent was right out of Brooklyn—not Jersey, not Queens, but Brooklyn. Ray knew it well. Tony was in his late twenties, and had greasy black hair and a thin, wiry build. In Brooklyn, Ray would have given this guy all the space he wanted, but this was *The Dim*, and he felt no obligation to be accommodating—at least, not before breakfast.

"So?" Ray said.

"Look, Brenda told me about some of the things you was sayin' about how stuff was different here, right?"

"Yeah." Ray said.

"It so happens that me and the boys were talking about some of the same things. We want you to come over to our table tonight. We get there at nine. Okay?"

"Maybe," Ray said.

"Good. I'll see ya tonight. Enjoy your breakfast," Tony said, as he got up and patted Ray on the shoulder.

The waitress put the breakfast plates on the table, and Ray gestured for her to refill his cup, again.

"You planning to run a marathon today?" she asked.

Ray just pointed to the cup.

Chapter 14

After breakfast Ray needed to walk, and think. Occasional light showers rolled over the island, a part of life in this corner of the world. In the absence of thunder, no one including Ray ran for cover.

As each shower passed, the sun came out and steam rose off the pavement — and Ray. He didn't mind. He was just glad to be outside, out of the car, and out of the motel, just walking and thinking about his existence thus far in *The Dim*.

From time to time he would stop and sit on an outcropping of coral rock, or a bench, to watch the waves break against the pilings of a pier.

In the late afternoon, he headed back toward Joe's. Brenda greeted him from behind the bar.

"Hi Ray. Getting an early start tonight?" she asked.

"No, just jonesing for a beer now. I'll be back later," Ray said, glancing in the direction of the table Tony and his friends had occupied.

"Good, but come in a little early, the boss whipped up some kick-ass chili."

"Sounds good. Will the ladies group be here, too?"

"You noticed them, too, did ya?"

Ray smiled, finished his beer, and got up. "Later."

Gary Ader

Chapter 15

Showered and shaved, Ray returned to Joe's by eight-thirty.

"Brenda, I'll try some of that chili you're pushing tonight, and a beer."

Brenda nodded, and within minutes, returned with his order.

"So, do I need to know what goes on at that table before I get involved?" he said.

"No, it's nothing really, just some guys who like to talk about what they find different here in *The Dim*. I just figure it's a 'guy thing'."

"And the other table, is that just a 'ladies thing'?"

"Yeah, kind of. Nothin' you would find interesting."

Ray wasted no time downing the chili. He ordered another beer and watched Brenda serve other customers.

Tony walked in with three other men and broke away to ask Ray to join them. "Come on over, and let me introduce you to the boys," he said.

"Glad you decided to join us Ray. My name is Matt. This is JC," he said, pointing to a Black man on his right. "This is Miguel, and you know Tony."

Matt appeared to be in his thirties, with long, dirty blond hair that hung oddly in pointed sections around his head like an upside down crown. His T-shirt had certainly seen better days, not unusual for the Keys, but it was his eyes that caught Ray's attention. They looked older than the rest of him. It made Ray feel uneasy, but he didn't know why. It was just a feeling, and this time the feeling came from his years as a spy, but he did remember Donald telling him to listen to his feelings.

"Brenda said you are the curious type," Matt said. "So are we. We only started getting together a few nights ago. We share experiences and try to figure out what *The Dim* is all about. "

"Sounds interesting. What kinds of things have you been able to put together so far?" Ray asked, again remembering Donald's admonitions.

"First, we've all traveled here from other places, and had different experiences. I'm trying to form a bigger picture, expand our horizons, and identify patterns," Matt said.

"Matt has been here the longest, over three-hundred solar cycles. He came from Boston. Miguel is from Texas, and JC is from Haiti. You know where I'm from," Tony said.

Something about JC intrigued Ray. He appeared to be in his thirties, but in *The Dim* age too, was relative. He was clean-shaven, including his head, and so black he was almost purple. His white T-shirt lit up his dark features and looked new, except for a small tear in the middle of his chest.

"What about you?" Matt asked. "Where did you travel from to get here?"

"I drove down from Richmond," Ray replied. "But what was that about solar cycles?"

"Maybe I was being over technical," Tony conceded. "I should have said days. Matt says we can tell that a day here is about the same twenty-four hours we know from the other world. We can tell by the way our diurnal pattern works. You know what that is, right?"

Now, Ray became wary of Tony. Way too much technical jargon for a guy from Brooklyn who never outgrew the street slang.

"Of course. That's our bio-rhythm, our wake-sleep pattern," Ray said.

"Right. We all pretty much experience that in the same way. Days, weeks, months, they're all constructs, ways of adding up time," Matt said. "A year is the interval it takes the earth to complete one cycle around the sun, three hundred and sixty-five days in the other world. We have no way of knowing if that is the same here. The best we can do for now is count solar cycles."

Suddenly the room shuddered. Beer rippled in the pitcher and glasses rattled behind the bar. Then it stopped.

"*Bondye!* Was that an earthquake?" JC asked.

"This island is coral rock on sand. There are no earthquakes here, and if it were, it would have lasted longer and felt different," Matt said.

When the rumble stopped, everyone in the bar got back to their drinking and conversation.

"Back to the point," Tony said. "Since you arrived in *The Dim*, what have you noticed that seems different?"

Ray thought for a moment. "Well, if you want to see a difference, look around. Do you see anything unusual?" Ray asked.

They all looked around and shook their heads. "No," Matt said. "What do *you* see?"

"Nothing. Nothing at all. On the surface everything looks the same, but it's not. Things are different," Ray said. "You can't always see the differences, but sometimes you can feel them. You all must have had experiences that felt just a little off, or maybe a *lot* off, haven't you?" *Like Biker Dude's girlfriend having to be redirected, or Abby moving in and out of other realities as if she was changing a shirt.*

"Sometimes, I can feel things are different," JC added.

"Thank you, Captain Obvious," Tony said.

They were all silent for a moment as they considered what Ray had said.

"Of course," Miguel said, getting back to the subject. "But these are things you're not supposed to discuss."

Matt and Tony nodded in agreement. JC glanced at Ray. "That's what I mean," he said. "Who said you can't discuss them?"

Again, Matt looked at each of them. "The person who told us the rules of *The Dim.*"

Suddenly, Ray understood. *Ding.* "A man approached me in Richmond, said he had to speak to me. He's the one that told me about all the rules *and* my mission. He called it a quest. He would never say where he got his instructions. His name was Donald Spade, and he said he was an attorney. I had a close relative I trusted, he was an attorney, too." Ray also remembered Juan and Biker Dude and their recognizable tattoos.

Matt looked at the others.

"Ya know the guy I met, Guido Molinari, reminded me of my cousin Rocco," said Tony. "There was a guy who could make a marinara sauce you could die for."

"Yvette duMonde, spoke to me," JC added. "She reminded me of my Aunt Mirasu, a Voodoo priestess."

"Eduardo Lopez," Miguel said looking at the others. "He was a truck driver, just like my brother Guillermo."

They looked at Matt.

"Ryan O'Flaherty, a police captain in Boston, just like my dad," he said, pausing and looking at Ray. "And that my new friend is why we wanted you to join us. Nobody sees everything, but if we each add a piece to the puzzle we can see a bigger picture. I'll have to think about this."

"Don't overthink. It's not that hard," Ray said, his tone harsher than he intended.

"Whadaya mean?" Tony asked.

"Can't you see? They chose *familiars*, people, or images we would trust so we would take them seriously. Every question I asked was answered with a certainty that came from a higher authority. 'I must speak with you,' or 'you must never do this or that,' or 'you may not,' 'it is the way of *The Dim*, and you must accept it.' Things like that."

"What's a familiar?" Tony asked.

Matt put his hand on his forehead. "Shit, I can't believe it. A familiar is an animal or person that carries out the wishes of a witch or wizard, or, in this case, I don't know what. That's the short version."

It was so clear that Ray couldn't understand why they hadn't figured it out. He watched the others slowly beginning to understand, and imagined little bells going off inside their heads. Or did they?

"And what else have you noticed that's different?" Tony pushed.

"From the other world?" Ray asked.

"What you are talking about is something we call *el otro mundo,* the other world. In other places they use different names. *The first world* is one, but there are others," Miguel said.

"Lot mond lan," JC added.

Tony and Miguel sat in silence, processing.

"So the answer begs the question: Who is running this dog and pony show?" Ray said.

"That, I am afraid is something we may never know. We receive information piecemeal, a little at a time, same as you. We may *think* we are making breakthroughs, but we only know what they want us to know," Matt said.

It wasn't *what* Matt said, but the way he said it that bothered Ray. It was with the same annoying sense of authority Donald used. Ray didn't think he was given information in bits and pieces. He thought of every encounter, or new piece of information, as part of a learning curve. Sometimes it felt like a roller coaster, but the result was the same.

Brenda set another pitcher of beer on the table. "Ray was right," she observed, "from over there you guys do look like conspirators."

Ray crumpled a paper napkin and tossed it at her, and she caught it in her left hand.

"Good catch," Ray said.

"I know another good catch," Brenda said, adding some extra sway to her hips as she walked back to the bar. That caused Ray to flush slightly. Matt looked at him, and Miguel and Tony made hooting noises.

"This opens up a whole new avenue of thought," Matt said. Each man began to re-examine the conversations they had with their *familiars*. "I think that's enough for tonight, Ray, join us tomorrow night, same time."

"Probably," Ray said, before walking over to the bar.

Brenda finished taking care of customers and restocking the bar, before she joined Ray.

"Was that an invitation?" Ray asked.

"I gave you your invitation when you first came in here. I told you I was off on Sundays and Mondays."

"But today is Thursday," Ray said, sounding like a little boy.

"Yes it is," she said, putting her finger on the tip of his nose. "That means you'll have to be patient for three more days."

Gary Ader

Chapter 16

Now one of the co-conspirators, Ray joined them the following night, hoping to find enlightenment. Instead, he found boredom. Matt, Tony, and Miguel got into a discussion of things long since settled in Ray's mind, and JC was expressing frustration at the superficial nature of their discussion.

Ray left them and went to the bar for another beer *and* to see Brenda.

"Hi, everything okay over there?" she asked.

"Not really. Sometimes they go off into the weeds. How are you doing?"

"Looking forward to my day off," she smiled.

"Me too."

Ray's attention was suddenly drawn to a customer at the end of the bar, a man in his thirties, who looked like he had been literally dragged through the mud. Nobody else seemed to notice or care, but Ray knew the meaning of the blank expression on his face. He was a new arrival.

The man finished his beer and stared into the empty glass. Ray looked toward Brenda to see if she would offer him a refill. When he looked back, a girl with long, stringy blond hair stood at his side. She had the same grungy appearance as the man, save for the strands of colorful beads around her neck. She pulled a small plastic bag from one of her pockets and put it on the bar between them.

His gaze shifted from his glass to the plastic bag and then to the girl. He smiled, and put his hand on the bag. She put her hand on his.

"Hey, Ray, you comin' back?" Tony called to him.

Ray looked toward the table. "Yeah, in a minute." When he looked back, the couple was walking out of the bar.

Is she his familiar? Ray wondered.

"Looks like that new guy got lucky, "Tony said, as Ray approached the table.

Ray said nothing, but looked at JC.

"I think I've had enough for tonight," JC said, as he got up.

"Okay, let's call it a night," Matt said.

Ray and JC walked out together. When they were clear of the bar, JC asked, "Do you think that guy got lucky, or was it something else?"

"Depends what you mean by lucky," Ray said.

"Do not play games with me, you know what I mean." JC was serious.

"Obviously, he was a fresh arrival," Ray said. "And she could be the *familiar* sent to greet him. They're going to smoke some of what was in that bag and then talk for a while, and then they'll probably get laid. So I guess he got lucky," Ray said.

"That's what I like about you Ray. You see things as they really are. Those baboons inside, they never see what is right under their noses. And they can talk for hours and say nothing."

"Or more likely they don't say what they see," Ray said. "And *that* is what I like about you, JC. You tell it like it is, but you don't tell everything. I think you know a lot more than the others, but you don't let on. Am I right?"

"Tomorrow, meet me at the diner for breakfast," JC said. "We can talk then.

Gary Ader

Chapter 17

In the other world, Ray was never was much of a breakfast eater, but, in The Dim, he was ravenous. JC was no different.

"What does JC stand for?" Ray asked.

"Jean Claude, but I never use that. JC suits me."

"And what about that?" Ray asked, pointing to JC's shirt. It was blue today, and looked new, except for the slit in the front.

"You are full of questions. We will have much to talk about, but that is something I do not wish to discuss now."

"Fair enough," Ray said. "Let's walk."

They walked down the street leading to the Hemingway house. About halfway there, Ray suddenly felt an uneasiness he hadn't experienced before in *The Dim*. He stopped.

"What is the matter?" JC asked, putting his hand on Ray's shoulder.

"Not sure, just a strange feeling, maybe nothing."

After another block, Ray stopped again. This time, he knew what the feeling was. "We're being followed."

JC did a careful 360 and saw nothing. "Do not get paranoid on me," he said. "All of this talk is getting to you, I think.

"No, not paranoid," Ray replied. "I know we are being followed, even if you can't see anyone. I'm sure of it. Look, it's kind of like the thing with your shirt. I don't want to explain it now. Okay?"

"Sure Ray. If you say so."

Across the street from Papa's house was a lighthouse, and beyond that a pier used by cruise ships and sometimes the Navy. There were no ships in port now, but Ray could clearly see three figures on the pier standing near one of the cement barriers. He pulled JC back behind the lighthouse.

"What?" JC asked.

"On the pier, I saw the newbie couple that was in the bar last night," Ray said.

"So, maybe we should talk to them?"

"Someone else is."

"Who?" JC said.

"Matt."

JC leaned around the corner of the building to look.

"That son of a bitch!" Ray said. "The man and woman are a couple, and Matt is their familiar. His little discussion group is just a con to get us to open up to him about what we have learned about *The Dim. He's a spy. Ding!*

JC leaned around the corner again. He saw Matt shaking hands with both the man and the woman.

"We must make sure he does not see us," JC said.

"Follow me." Ray ducked inside the doorway to the lighthouse and began climbing, JC right behind him.

"So that is what you sensed?" JC asked

"No, there has been someone else following us since we left the diner. He must be good, because I haven't spotted him yet."

From the top of the lighthouse they could see Matt walking down the street toward the bar. The couple remained on the pier, sitting on the barrier holding on to each other.

"What do you think we should do?" Ray asked.

"I think we should offer them some friendship," JC said, pulling a rolled marijuana cigarette from his pocket.

They slowly made their way down the steps to the bottom of the lighthouse. As they stepped into the street, they saw Matt reach the end of the block and turn the corner.

The couple eyed Ray and JC warily as they approached.

"I'm Ray and this is JC," he said, as they walked toward the shade.

"I'm Smokey and this is Starla."

"You two look like you need to relax," JC said to them, the joint visible in his hand.

"We understand you've been through a lot, and I suspect that the man you just spoke to did not leave you feeling much better," Ray said.

They nodded in agreement.

"Why don't we go to the lighthouse and relax under those trees. It will be cooler and we can talk," JC said gesturing with the reefer.

"The man who just spoke to you, what was his name?" Ray asked.

"Matt, Matt Schroeder, I think," Smokey said. Starla nodded.

"Did he remind you of anyone you knew in the other world?" JC asked.

The man and woman looked at each other.

"He sort of did," Starla said.

"Ya know, he *did* remind me of Ernie," Smokey said. "Really cool dude. A couple of hits on a bong, and Ernie could see all the truth in the world that nobody else could."

"We call that a *familiar*," Ray said. "They send someone that reminds you of someone you trust. He probably said he had to tell you things, and those things were the rules of what you cannot do here in *The Dim*. Is that about right?"

They both nodded.

There was something else that had been on Ray's mind since he first saw them, and he had to ask one of the forbidden questions. JC passed the joint to Smokey.

"What were you doing before you got here, to *The Dim*?" Ray asked. "I know what Matt told you, but this is really important."

Starla nodded.

"Things were getting tough up in Boston," Smokey said. "And we needed a change, so we came down to the Keys just to, ya know chill out. We were here for only a few weeks, when somebody said there was a hurricane out in the ocean somewhere, and we should probably get out. We didn't know where to go, so we stayed. We were in a little house on the east end of the island, and were just getting mellow, when it was like a bomb went off, and everything went flying. I tried to hold on to Starla, but she got pulled away. The next thing I remember is being on the street and walking into the bar where Starla found me."

"How long was it until you found yourselves here?" Ray asked.

"Matt said we were wandering around for a day, in shock, I guess, before we found the bar," Starla said.

"JC, what happened two nights ago?" Ray asked, knowing the answer.

"Shit, that was the night we felt the whole bar shake," JC replied. We thought it might be an earthquake."

Smokey and Starla looked at Ray, but he didn't elaborate.

"Do you guys have any money for food and new clothes?" JC asked.

"Yes," Starla said. "When Matt saw us the night we arrived, he said we will always have enough money for what we need. He said we could go back to the house we were in, but I'm not sure I want to do that. Besides, how come everything is okay now?"

"Because that was the other world," JC said, "and now you are in *The Dim*. Things may look the same on the surface, but things here are not always going to be as you expect.

"Did Matt say anything to you about being on a quest of some kind?" Ray asked.

"No, nothing like that at all," Smokey answered.

"But Miguel did, but I'm not supposed to talk about it," Starla added.

"When did you see Miguel?" JC asked.

"Last night after we left the bar," Starla replied. "We were out here all night. He showed up around sunrise."

"That's okay, but did Miguel tell you some of the same things Matt did?"

"Yeah, and Matt seemed angry when we told him how we already knew. I don't know why, we didn't do anything," Starla said.

Ray stood up. "Don't worry about it."

"When we saw Matt this morning we didn't want to talk to him, but he said he just wanted to see if we were okay," Smokey said.

"Why don't you get some food and rest," Ray said. "This is a small island. We'll see you later. Will you two be okay?"

"Yeah, as long as we are together," Smokey said. The couple stood up, and he put his arm around Starla.

"And try not to smoke any more today," Ray said. "You need to get your heads straight."

The couple looked at JC and Ray, still disoriented in *The Dim,* and not understanding why everybody seemed so interested in them.

Ray watched them walk away. Smokey was head and shoulders taller than Starla. He held her close as they walked. In either world he didn't think they could manage without each other.

"So Matt is not their familiar, but Miguel is?" JC asked.

"I think so," Ray said. He saw movement behind one of the windows in the Hemmingway house and added, "I don't want to hang around here. Let's go back to my room."

Chapter 18

The air this time of day had a pleasant softness, and Ray didn't want to be indoors. But he desperately needed to confer with JC, and they needed privacy.

They sat on the balcony of Ray's room. Usually, it was never too early for a drink, but now he wanted a clear head. The toke he took off the joint they shared with Smokey and Starla had worn off. Ray felt the muscles in his neck and back tighten. Things in *The Dim* were starting to get complicated.

When he left The Rest Inn, he thought all he would have to do was travel around searching for wisdom, like it was fruit he could pluck off a tree. He was learning that life in this world was at least as complicated as the one he left behind. He hypothesized that all of the human motivations he had known to exist in the other world were also present here. The difference was a lack of permanence — his own nomadic state for one, and the seemingly temporary nature of the existence of everyone else he encountered.

He remembered Darlene thanking Abby for coming back to help him remember the accident. But where did she come back *from*? And when she moved on, where did she go? Those were questions he might never get the answers to, but one thing was certain: There were spies in *The Dim*. But why?

They sat in silence for a few minutes, enjoying the air and watching the calm water.

"So now we know that Matt was pretending to be a familiar, as you call it, and his little discussion group is a way of spying on us to see what we know," JC said.

"Apparently so, but I can't figure what his game is. Any knowledge about *The Dim* that we have he can find out for himself. He has nothing to gain with this charade. Does he just get off screwing with people? I don't get it."

"Maybe, it is just some kind of power trip. Perhaps, he wants to make others see him as important, or maybe he is just a bully," JC said.

"Either way, don't forget that Tony has a part in this. I saw him in the window of the Hemmingway house. I can't be sure, but I think he was just covering Matt's back, and he *did* see us," Ray said, an uneasy feeling forming in his stomach.

"But, does he know that you have seen *him*?" JC said with a big toothy smile.

"Probably not. So for now we have that advantage," Ray said.

"And now we know that Miguel is the familiar for the young couple."

"We still don't know if we can be sure of that, or if he is any threat to us.'

"That is true. But what do you make of the other thing?"

"I think, the earth tremor we felt at the bar, here in *The Dim*, coincides with a strong hurricane hitting this location in the other world. Smokey and Starla confirmed that," Ray said.

"That would mean that the boundary between the two worlds may be delicate, or may just be thinner in some places. Does that make sense?" JC asked.

"Yes it does," Ray replied. "And if we felt the impact of the storm here, then maybe some of what happens here can be felt in the other world.

JC looked troubled and fingered the tear in his shirt, which was now larger. "I have to go."

"What's up?" Ray asked.

"I feel uneasy, and, when I do, there is someone I need to speak with."

"You mean someone besides your ol' buddy Ray?"

"Yes. We will skip the meeting tonight. I want you to come with me. Meet me at the lighthouse at eight-thirty."

"Sure, but make it nine. That's when Matt and Tony will be at the bar. We still don't know about Miguel, so be careful, and take the back way to Truman Street."

JC paused and locked eyes with Ray. In that instant, each man knew he could trust the other.

"See you later," he said, and left.

And what about Brenda, can I trust her?

Gary Ader

Chapter 19

Ray knew JC lived in a boarding house at the north end of Eaton Street, just across from the Tailfin Bar. At eight-thirty, he walked into the Tailfin. The crowd there was a little more rugged. The kind of place where Biker Dude would hang out.

Taking a vantage point at a table in the back, he had a clear view of the boarding house through the front window. He ordered a beer and tried to relax, since it would be a while till their meeting. A football game was playing on one of the TV screens over the bar, on the other was a NASCAR race. Neither one could hold his attention for long, but something else did. A young woman sat at a high top table across from the bar. It wasn't her looks that attracted his attention. It was her isolation.

Since arriving in *The Dim*, she was the first person Ray had seen holding a cell phone. She stared at the screen and pressed buttons, changing apps, or texting, he guessed. Not even the cheers and boos of the crowd watching the televisions caused her to look away from her phone. Nothing else was worthy of her attention. She was in a bubble, completely disengaged from her surroundings. *Perhaps it's her way of coping with the shock of having died in the other world, or does it have something to do with her quest?*

Those thoughts and a few beers kept Ray occupied until nine-fifteen, when he saw JC leave the boarding house and walk away from Duval Street toward one of the darker back streets.

Ray left the bar and followed him, keeping in the shadows and leaving nearly two blocks between them. As JC approached the lighthouse, Ray ducked behind a palm tree. Nothing moved in the still night air. The only sounds were those of the waves hitting the sea wall. He felt safe.

He saw JC looking back in his direction.

"Were you following me?" JC asked.

"No, I just wanted to make sure you weren't being followed."

"And who had *your* back?" JC looked angry.

"Look, I'm going with you to meet some mystery person. I know there are at least two people out there who are watching us. I have to be careful."

"Very well," JC said, "perhaps we should have shared some of our secrets before? I think we should later."

"Agreed."

"The person we are going to see is Queen Rowena Jones. She is one of the most powerful practitioners of voodoo magic. She knows much and sees things we cannot."

"Voodoo in *The Dim*?"Ray questioned. "Now, there's a twist I wouldn't have expected."

"You will be in the presence of strong magic. You must show respect at all times, and you will address her as Queen Rowena. Do you understand?"

"Yes."

"Do not let her think that you do not believe in voodoo, or she will shrink your head and put it on her bedpost!" JC said

"What?!" Ray winced.

"Ha ha," JC laughed, showing his big white smile. "Just messing with you. Let's go," he said, putting his arm around Ray. "You have too much on your mind. It is bad for you."

Ray was not at all amused. True he didn't believe in magic, or a hereafter, for that matter, but here he was, in *The Dim*, so he considered this new situation carefully, and with that realization, once again heard the little bell in his head. *Ding*.

They walked several blocks, then ducked through a narrow space behind some tall hedges. There, hidden from street view, stood a bungalow that sat well back on the property.

"This place is completely dark. Are you *sure* somebody is in there?" Ray asked in a whisper.

JC gestured for him to follow. They made their way to the windowless front door, and JC knocked twice, then once, then three times. The door opened, and a widening sliver of light was the only greeting they received. JC entered first. Ray closed the door behind them. The smell of incense was strong and strangely calming. The smoke from burning candles and incense made their vision hazy, as they approached the beaded curtains in a doorway.

"Come," a female voice, deep and smooth, with a thick Creole accent, beckoned them. Cautiously, they threaded their way through the curtains into the next room, smaller than the one they first entered. Again, JC went first. Ray took in as much of the room as he could. The walls were covered with tapestries and animal skins, and symbols of voodoo magic surrounded them. Bones, feathers, snakeskins, and other fetishes of the craft were randomly placed on tables and shelves. Several glass cylinders contained eyeballs that seemed to follow their movement.

Heavy cloth embroidered with strange symbols was draped over the table in the center of the room. Behind it sat a large woman, skin as black as JC's. Her head was covered in red and purple scarves, voodoo colors for power and spirituality. With outstretched arms, she gestured for them to sit opposite her. Her dark eyes sat so deeply in her head, they would have seemed non-existent were it not for the reflection of the candlelight.

They sat silently as she regarded Ray.

"Why are you here?" she asked, turning her head to JC.

"I am here because I feel an uneasy presence within myself, and for my friend, his name is — "

"I *know* his name. Raymond Walker, tell me why you are here," she said, turning to him.

"Queen Rowena, I am a seeker of knowledge and wisdom."

"And do you believe in voodoo?"

"I admit to having no knowledge of the voodoo arts. I am here to learn. I beg you not to interpret my ignorance as any manner of disrespect."

"Jean Claude, I like this friend of yours, he does not try to bullshit me like the others."

"Thank you, Queen Rowena. My friend has many questions, and I have faith that you will be able to help him find his way in this world."

"I *know* his questions. First we must have a drink. The sharing will bring us closer."

She stood up, revealing an imposing physical presence. From a cabinet she removed a tray with a pitcher and three glasses, put it on the table, and filled each of the glasses before sitting down.

In the dim light, the liquid in the glass appeared as black as her skin.

Ray looked at the glass with apprehension.

"Drink." she said.

Eye of newt, toe of frog.

"Not quite," she said seeming to read his mind. "If you wish to find knowledge, you must drink."

He knew it was a test. She wanted to see if he trusted her.

She lifted her glass, JC lifted his, and Ray followed suit. He looked at Rowena and JC. They were motionless and silent, waiting for him to drink first. He put the glass to his lips and drank. Then JC and Rowena drank from their glasses.

To Ray's surprise the room did not spin, and no hallucinations hijacked his consciousness.

"It's good," Ray said without thinking.

"It is actually a recipe for sangria I found in *Good Housekeeping*," Rowena said.

Ray and JC looked at each other, surprised by her wry humor.

"Raymond, place your hands on the table, palms up."

Ray complied and watched as she traced the lines in his palm with her long purple fingernail. First one hand, then the other, before leaning back in her chair. She tilted her head, and contemplated what she saw.

"This is very strange. I see that you have had three lives, very strange indeed. Is this true?"

Was his lifetime with Abby really another life? thought Ray. How could she know?

"It is true. After I arrived in *The Dim,* there was this girl, a woman and she—"

"I know about her," Rowena said. "And there will be other women, but none of them will be like Abby," Rowena said.

Ray had no idea how she could know what happened at The Rest Inn. He would have thought the mention of Abby would have stirred emotions within him, but it didn't. His recollection lacked any emotional content, and the realization of this fact troubled him.

"And you will have more lives at the end of your journey."

"Is that when I will move on?" Ray asked.

"Possibly. It is hard to see." She took another drink of wine. "I see your destiny splitting into two paths. I cannot be sure of the meaning. I have never seen this before. There is a path that will lead you to another life in this world, but it will not be like the one you had with Abby. It will be very different, but I cannot see exactly what it will be. The images are fuzzy and dark. I do not think it will be a bad thing, in fact, it may be what you have wanted all along. There is another line that branches off from the first. On that path you must move on."

"Thank you, Queen Rowena," Ray said. "I wish I understood more. Is there anything else you can tell me?"

Rowena did not answer at first. She refilled her glass. "JC, take some more, and refill Raymond's glass."

JC did as she asked. They sat quietly for a while, taking sips of wine, while Rowena seemed to commune with the spirit world.

"There are some things you must be aware of before you leave here. I know you have identified two men you do not trust. Your judgment of them is valid, but they have no powers in *The Dim*. They ignore their quest and bully others. They are *manje pompous*. The woman you have met, you can trust her, but not too much. Enjoy her, but do not delay your journey because of her. I think she will tell you that, as well."

JC muffled a laugh, and Ray looked at him.

He was looking forward to his time with Brenda and welcomed the reassurance.

"You said you seek knowledge and wisdom," Rowena said.

Ray nodded.

"Then I will tell you that you must learn to give of yourself if you want others to do the same." She took another drink. Her gaze shifted upward as she spoke. "Your ability to do this will be tested. Many of the things you did not accept as real in *lot mond lan*, things that were the stuff of myth and superstition, are very real in *The Dim*. You must be willing to accept this unconditionally if you are to succeed in your quest. Does that frighten you?"

"No, I don't think so, but I'm not sure I understand," Ray said.

"The fabric between the two realms is very thin in some places," Rowena said. "It is why you felt a shock here when the water destroyed this place in the other world. It is why some see apparitions and ghosts in the other world and why . . . why you must accept the realities you find in this world as improbable as they may seem."

When she finished speaking, a long silence followed. However, the time was not wasted, as Ray considered her words and consciously chose to believe absolutely in what she said. In fact, he took comfort from them. It was not an act of faith, it was a realization. He had already seen enough of *The Dim* to know the rules here were very different. Ray thought this new awareness would have set off church bells in his head, but again only the smallest *ding* was heard.

"Now Raymond, there is something you must do for me," Rowena said, placing a scissors on the table. "Cut off a piece of your hair, just a small piece, and give it to me."

Ray paused. He remembered her words about giving and receiving, and seeing no reason to refuse, took the scissors and did as she asked. Rowena went to one of the many cabinets in the room, took out a small, black, wax figure of a man, and a white ribbon. She took the piece of hair and pushed it into the head of the figure and tied the white ribbon around its neck, then placed it on a shelf with many other dolls of different colors.

"The doll is black, the color that repels enemies and negative energy. The white ribbon represents success. Raymond, adding your hair to the doll will give these protections to you. By giving me what I asked, of your own free will, you have demonstrated your belief in what I have told you. To honor your trust in me, it is my duty to protect this doll with my life. However, even I will someday have to move on. When that happens, you will no longer be under the protection of my magic. Continue your quest, and do not waste time."

"Queen Rowena, thank you for sharing your wisdom, and for your protection. I will not forget your words," Ray said.

"Now for you, Jean Claude. I understand the reason for your uneasiness. It is the lack of any progress in your quest. The tear in your shirt grows larger. You cannot allow this to continue. You must make an effort. Perhaps it is time you sought help from another," she said, tilting her head toward Ray.

JC was about to ask another question when Rowena spoke. "Jean Claude, Raymond, our time together is done. You must leave now." She waved her hand in the air making a circle.

Ray half expected her to disappear in a cloud of smoke, but she didn't.

"Queen Rowena, *mesi ak deni ou*," JC said.

In the other room Ray noticed the candles were nearly completely burned down. JC opened the door. Daylight blinded them. With hands in front of their eyes, they closed the door behind them.

"JC were we in there all night? What was in that wine?"

"Voodoo magic is very strong. It can even affect time."

"I guess. What was that you said to her before we left?"

"It was Creole for thank you and bless you," JC said.

"And what was that other thing she said about Matt and Tony?" Ray asked.

JC laughed. "That was Creole too. She said they were shit heads."

Chapter 20

It was Saturday, so Ray and JC decided to get some rest. They agreed to meet again that evening at the Tailfin. Neither wanted to return to Matt's discussion group. Ray remembered that Brenda's nights off were Sunday and Monday. He needed to go to Joe's early to talk to her first.

"Where ya been? I thought you and JC decided to blow this place?" Brenda said.

"No, we've just been hanging out. Matt's little group got boring. *Not really a lie.* So, tomorrow is our big date?"

"Date!" she laughed. "Okay we can call it that."

"No, seriously, I figured you'd want to get some rest tomorrow during the day, and then we could go out to dinner, to the Starfish, if that's okay with you," Ray said.

"And I thought chivalry was dead. Ya got class Ray. Sure, pick me up about five. I live in the purple house up the street from Hemingway's."

"Then we have a date."

She waved him away. "Tomorrow."

Ray felt good for the first time in what seemed like a very long time. Walking in the cooler evening air he wished for the feeling to last.

JC was waiting in front of the Tailfin, and they walked toward the table Ray had occupied the night before.

A hand gripped each man's shoulder. Ray looked around, and saw Matt and Tony behind them.

"It looks like you two have been busy avoiding us," Matt said.

"They've been busy sneakin' around, following us maybe," Tony said.

"Look guys—" Ray started to say, as Matt pushed him down into the chair nearest the wall.

JC chose not to resist as Tony pushed him into the other chair.

Matt and Tony occupied the other two seats, blocking any attempts to leave. Their backs were to the room. *A very bad position*, Ray thought.

"How about we keep this conversation friendly, and you two just tell us what the hell you've been up to," Tony demanded.

"It's like I told you in the beginning," Matt added, "we just want to share information."

"So what kind of information do you want to share with us?" Ray asked defiantly.

"That's not the way it works. First you tell us," Tony said.

"Well, first of all I don't think we should be having this conversation."

"Well," Matt said with a smirk, "I think we *should*, and I don't have all night, so why don't you just begin."

"In that case," Ray said, "I think you should never sit with your back to the door."

Before Matt and Tony could look around, a large hand grasped each of them by the shoulder. Miguel towered over them from behind. They tried to stand and break loose, but Miguel had an iron grip on them. Watching them try to move reminded Ray of the way

Donald gripped his arm the night Biker Dude roughed up Darlene.

"When I didn't see my two *amigos* at Joe's tonight I knew I should find them before they got themselves into more trouble," Miguel said.

"No trouble man, just talking to my buds here, that's all," Matt said.

"Yeah, no trouble here. Why don't you just go find a senorita or something?" Tony said.

"Enough! You two are finished here. You have interfered with the quests of others and failed to begin your own," Miguel said, as he effortlessly raised them to their feet, and pushed them toward the doorway.

"Hey man, what are ya doin?" asked Tony.

"*Andale come mierdes,*" said Miguel, pushing them forward.

When they were gone, Ray and JC felt a sense of relief. Matt and Tony hadn't frightened them, but neither was up for a fight tonight, and Miguel had arrived just in time.

"That was Rowena's protection," JC said.

"Sure," Ray said, skeptically.

"What did you expect, for them to vanish in a cloud of smoke? Voodoo is very strong magic, but sometimes it has to be subtle."

"Okay," Ray said, realizing that he had begun to truly believe. *Ding!*

"What did Miguel say to them?" JC asked.

"He called them shit heads."

Gary Ader

Chapter 21

Ray bought another round and brought the drinks back to the table. "I bought first, so you talk first. What's your story?"

JC sat quietly, appearing to stare into space, but Ray could tell his gaze was inward.

"What I am going to tell you I have never told to anyone—not in *lot mond lan,* and not in *The Dim.* You have asked about the cut in the shirts I wear . . ."

Ray nodded.

"It is the guilt I carry. My quest is to rid myself of that guilt. When I do, the tear will no longer appear in every shirt I wear. That is what Yvette duMonde, my familiar said. She knew, even though I never told her."

JC took another drink. His eyes were damp.

"It was a long time ago, in Haiti. They were bad days. The *Tonton Macutes* roamed the streets. They did whatever they wanted, and there was no one who could stop them. Do you know about the *Tonton*?"

Ray nodded. They were supposed to be a type of police, but, in fact, were ruthless gangs who preyed on the people.

"One night I was walking home after drinking with friends. It was very dark. The only light was from the moon. I heard a girl screaming, and followed her sound. I found her behind a building, with a man on top of her, raping her. I tried to pull him off her, but he fought me and pulled out a knife. It was so dark I only saw the reflection of the blade in the moonlight. We struggled in the dirt, until I grabbed the knife and, without thinking, put it into his chest." JC pointed to the tear in his shirt.

"But that wasn't murder," Ray said. "You were saving the girl and your own life."

"Perhaps, *mon ami,* but it was only after I had killed him that I saw his face." JC fought to hold back tears. "He was my brother."

"Shit."

"When my mother received the news of his death, she was heartbroken. I could never bring myself to tell her what had happened. Two years later, we had the earthquake. Our house collapsed on us. We died in the same room, at the same time. Yvette told me I would not find her in *The Dim,* at least not until I was free of my guilt. She said that when I forgave myself, my mother would forgive me too. At first I did not understand, in the other world, she never knew, maybe here in *The Dim* she does."

"Now that you have told me, how do you feel?" Ray asked, hoping JC heard a little bell in his head.

"Saying those words was very hard. Right now I do not know."

"You saved the girl, and, if you didn't kill him, he most certainly would have killed you. Do you think he would have felt any guilt about that?"

"Probably not."

"And, if he had killed you that night in the dark, do you think it would have been any easier on your mother?" Ray asked.

"No, but at least she never knew that he was one of the *Tonton Macutes.*"

"Do you think the girl was the first one he had attacked, or would have been the last? You saved more than one girl. You know what the *Tonton* did. You saved many people from harm," Ray said softly. "Think about it while I get us another round."

When Ray returned and put the glasses on the table, he noticed the tear in JC's shirt was smaller. The two men drank in silence. JC wiped his eyes with one hand while gripping his shirt with the other. Ray could see JC knew his words were true.

Gary Ader

Chapter 22

It was getting late, and the crowd at the Tailfin Bar started to thin out. The usual din had subsided. "And now my friend, you *must* have something you wish to share with me," JC said.

Ray sat pensively. Hearing JC's story had made him reflect more carefully on his own tale, and do what he had never done before: question his choices, and ponder possible outcomes.

"My story also involves a knife, a young woman, and a killing," Ray began. It came out easier than he expected.

JC watched Ray thinking of how to begin.

"I can't tell you how long ago it's been. *The Dim* has distorted my sense of time, but it was during the height of the Cold War between the United States and The Soviet Union. Do you remember that?"

"I was only a boy, and we were so poor that my mother and father spent almost every day finding food and clean water. Even so, my mother insisted I go to school. I remember the teacher telling us about the *super puissance*, what you call the super powers, America and Russia. They had bombs that could kill everyone on earth. As children in Haiti that was too big an idea for us to understand," JC said.

"Part of what I did was to try to prevent that from happening," Ray said.

"Were you in the military?" JC asked.

"No. I was a spy."

"Like James Bond!" said JC, referring to the Ian Fleming character.

"No, I worked for a secret organization that reported directly to the President of the United States. I was sent to Paris. My mission was to receive information from our assets, other spies, and bring it back to America."

"That sounds very dangerous. Were you afraid?"

"No. I probably should have been, but I wasn't. On a previous mission, I was in Moscow. After being literally behind enemy lines, and being followed by the KGB, I didn't think Paris would pose any unusual problems."

"I would think not," JC said. "Paris is wonderful any time of year, and, in *The Dim*, it is only a three hour flight from Miami"

"Well, as it turns out, the East German secret service, Stazi, was also involved in operations there. That became a problem when the asset I was receiving information from got careless. 'Bad tradecraft' we call it. She saw a woman nearby when she gave me an envelope. She should have aborted the handoff, but she didn't, and I failed to catch her mistake. The woman in question, Natalie, was stalking my contact. She overheard one of our passwords and saw her put the envelope in my pocket."

"Did you know what was in the envelope?" JC asked.

"Not exactly, just that it concerned France's developmental plans for nuclear weapons."

"That is serious business," JC said.

"Yes, and that is why the East Germans and the Soviets wanted it. Two days later, I saw Natalie at a luncheon. She had already contacted her Stazi friends, who planned to kidnap me as I left the building. I managed to avoid them by taking another exit with Natalie, who agreed to walk with me to see some of the city sights after dark. She even offered sex in exchange for the envelope."

"Was that a hard choice?" JC smiled.

"Absolutely not. The mission always comes first, and real spies, if they are smart, almost never sleep with the enemy."

"You mean it is not like in the James Bond movies?"

"No my friend, not at all. Anyway, I knew that if our business was not concluded that night, the two East German agents would find me, and it would be game over."

Ray had to pause. It had been many years ago, in the other world, and he was surprised how vivid his memories were. Most of his recollections of his life in the other world had already faded to sepia images.

"I considered my options," Ray continued. "Giving her the envelope was not one of them. Going to the police was not an option either. I would have blown my cover and would have endangered many other assets."

"You were in a very difficult position," JC acknowledged.

"Yes, so I decided the only way to end the problem was to end Natalie. We walked down to the Seine to see the Eiffel Tower. In the shadow of a bridge she kissed me, and, as she did, I plunged a knife into her. Her eyes were open when the last breath left her body, and I let her fall into the river."

"*Bo lan mouri.* The kiss of death."

"A little dramatic, but basically yes. The strange part was when she pulled me toward her she had only one hand on my shoulder. Usually a woman puts both arms around a man when she kisses."

"That was murder!" JC said.

"No it wasn't. We were adversaries, soldiers in a Cold War."

"But killing like that with a knife while your lips were together, I cannot imagine such a thing," JC said leaning away from Ray.

They barman rang the bell for "last call", but Ray continued. "Do you know why she had only one arm around me when we kissed?"

"No."

"When they recovered her body two weeks later they found a knife in her pocket. She was holding it when she kissed me. Yes, the kiss of death."

"But you did not know that when you murdered her."

"What part of this aren't you getting? Had I hesitated, or tried for a second kiss, she would have killed me. And, by the way, the word is *killed*, not murdered."

"Is there a difference?"

"Certainly. This wasn't a street mugging. We were both soldiers. Soldiers kill, they don't murder."

"Does that distinction give you comfort?"

"There is no comfort in killing, but it was necessary — to protect the envelope and my mission," Ray said, not really answering the question.

"Was there no other way for you? Couldn't you have just gone to the airport and left Paris?"

Those were the words Ray didn't want to hear. It was never his style to cut and run. When he was a kid in Brooklyn he decided confronting bullies was better than running from them. To Ray, Stazi were just bullies, so running away was not an option to be considered. This was the fatal flaw in Ray's character. In this case it was fatal for Natalie, and Ray never realized that he was favored more by luck than calculation. Now, in *The Dim*, he realized that this other choice would have protected his mission *and* he would not have killed — no — he would not have *murdered* Natalie. He felt a pain he had never known before. Remorse.

"It was the one option I had not considered until much later," Ray said. "Back then, running was a choice I never could have made. Once I found a solution to my problem, I didn't consider other alternatives. Years later, I realized the other choice I could have made. My mission would be safe and no lives would be lost. That realization put a black spot on my heart that I carried for the rest of my life."

"I think even longer," JC said quietly.

"I think you are right," Ray conceded. "I know now that I didn't have to kill her. I panicked. At the time, she was a problem, and I just wanted to get rid of her. It *was* murder." *Ding.*

It was the first time Ray had actually admitted his singular act of violence was wrong.

"There is one other thing," Ray continued. "The envelope contained information that helped the president persuade the Soviets to agree to the SALT treaty, limiting nuclear proliferation. That treaty potentially saved millions of lives."

"And you could have saved one more," JC added.

Chapter 23

Ray's walk to Brenda's house was filled with the anxiety of a high school boy on his first date. For all practical purposes it might very well have been. The last girl he dated was Wendy, his wife in the other world. His sense of time was no longer as reliable as it used to be, but he knew it was over fifty years ago, although it could have been much longer.

His once vivid recollection of that night was no longer clear, and lacked emotional content. He began to realize that his memories of life in the other world were slowly being replaced by new ones from *The Dim*. It was as if each new experience replaced one from his old life. To experience new things he had to give up part of himself, his past. He couldn't be sure, but he sensed it was not a random process. Queen Rowena had told him his quest for knowledge would involve his willingness to give in order to receive. It seemed like a metaphor when she said it. Now he realized it was real, and beyond his control—well, sort of. He could sit in his motel room and do nothing except cherish old memories from the other world. But Ray Walker would *never* make that choice. *Ding.*

Ray knew he had to move forward, and wondered if it was similar to the tugging Abby felt when she had to move on. All he knew was that it wasn't his time to move on yet. The pulling must be his quest.

The sight of Brenda in the orange glow of the late afternoon sun broke his train of thought. She sat on the front porch looking out over the water. She didn't see him approach, so he had time to look at her. She was radiant.

She smiled when she saw Ray, and walked down the stairs to meet him. He plucked a dandelion from the front yard and gave it to her.

"Thank you," she said, as she tucked it into her hair above her ear.

"It matches your dress."

"And look at you," she said, noticing he had given up his faded tee shirt and baggy shorts for a Hawaiian shirt and casual slacks.

They were like high school kids on a first date, and laughed at themselves. Right now, she just wanted to enjoy the sweetness of a first date, and he was caught up in her enjoyment of the moment. However, they were both adults, and knew how they wanted the evening to end.

She took his arm and they walked toward the Starfish. The late afternoon breeze was soft, and their shadows lengthened, as the sun got closer to the water. Brenda played tour guide, telling him about the history of the old buildings they passed. At The Rest Inn, Donald had told Ray there was no heaven. Right now, he disagreed.

Ray found the only white linen restaurant on the island, and requested a window table overlooking the water. They ordered cocktails, and after they made their menu selections, Brenda chose the dinner wine.

"How long have you been here?" Ray asked.

"*Here*, here, or here in Key West?" Brenda asked, echoing Ray's answer to her question the evening he arrived.

"Both."

"Well, I've been in Key West almost all of the time I've been in *The Dim*, but I can't remember exactly how long that is. Do you think that's weird?"

"Weird is normal here, so I would say that it sounds perfectly normal. If you asked me, I'd have to give you the same answer."

"Why do you think that is?"

"I suspect the reason is different for each of us, but mechanically, if that's the right word, it all kind of works the same way. It's like everybody has a watch. Each watch looks different, but inside they all have to do the same thing to show the correct time. Does that make any sense to you?" Ray asked.

"I think so. One thing I've learned working at Joe's is that even though we are all in the same place, everybody is here for a different reason . . . but I don't know if we should talk about that," Brenda said.

Their server brought their food, and the sommelier poured their wine. When they were alone again, Ray raised his glass and saw the candlelight reflected in her eyes. "To you and our time together."

She raised her glass. "Yes, and to our time together, here-here." She giggled, then they touched glasses before tasting their wine. After her second glass of wine Brenda said, "You know when I first met you I thought you were management."

"What?"

"Management, you know, like Miguel and the woman who told me why I was here, and the people that make all the rules," Brenda said.

"Really? Why would you think that?"

"Because you were new, and, like I said, you just take everything in, and you seem so . . . so confident. I think that's it, like you knew your way around even though you were new."

Ray was used to drinking beer or whiskey. The wine affected him differently, and he was feeling a little loose. "That's because I did a lot of traveling and had to acclimate to new surroundings quickly. It was part of my job as a spy." He was sorry he said the last part.

"Wow, really? Like James Bond?"

"No, not at all like that. Espionage is usually not as exciting as the movies."

"But, did you ever have to kill anyone?" Brenda asked, wide eyed.

Shit! Now how am I going to get out of this?

"I could tell you, but then I would have to kill you," he laughed, and then refilled her glass, before changing the subject. "To tell you the truth, I thought *you* might be management. Tending bar, you get to see and speak with almost everyone who comes into Joe's."

"What changed your mind?"

"Did I say I changed my mind?" He was about to go out on a very long limb. One that could wreck the entire evening. He had no choice. Something remembered from very long ago. He had to know if she was a honey trap. "How did you know about Miguel?"

"Oh, that. Miguel was here long before I got to the Keys. I've seen the way he talks to people, and he always seems to show up in time to prevent trouble from happening. Does that make sense?"

Ray could see she was being genuine, and he had seen how Miguel appeared in time to handle Matt and Tony, just when things started to heat up at the Tailfin.

"Yes, it does, and by the way, I did change my mind, because you just seemed too nice to be one of them. Even my familiar wasn't particularly pleasant."

"Well that's good. Then we can talk," Brenda said.

"I think we should."

She took another sip of wine. Ray could see through her demure expression. She hadn't planned on going down this path, but she had, and now Ray considered it fair game

"There's one thing I've wondered about since I got here," he said. "My fate is to be a homeless nomad on a quest. Some people I've met, like you, have jobs they go to every day. Why do you do it?"

"Nobody forces me to, if that's what you mean. I work at Joe's because I want to. It's kind of like part of what you called a quest, only for me it is a do-over."

"A what?"

"A do-over. My life in the other world kind of sucked. I had a bad childhood. People did bad things to me. When I got older, I did bad things to other people. Not the same kind of things, but I just wasn't a nice person."

"I'm sorry. I never would have guessed that about you."

"Yeah, so now I get a chance to start over, without the baggage. I guess you could say it is my quest to forget all of the bad things from the other world and become another version of myself here, a better one. So, working at Joe's I just get to be a regular person. I can't remember most of the bad stuff anymore. Now, I just get to be me. So how am I doing?"

Ding. "I think you're doing great. I like this version of you."

Brenda blushed. "Okay, okay. Enough about me, what kind of quest thingy are you on? Are you searching for the Holy Grail or something?"

"Nothing like that. I am a seeker of wisdom and knowledge, or is it knowledge and wisdom? I've had too much wine."

"And how do you know when you've found it?" Brenda asked.

"Well . . ." Ray rubbed his chin, "I hear a little bell in my head." *That sounded stupid!*

Brenda laughed. "Are you kidding me?"

"No it's the truth," Ray said, raising his right hand. "In the other world I had a family and a job, well, two jobs really, and I never bothered to pay much attention to life and its bigger questions, or to think about other people and how they fit into the grand scheme of things. When you told me your story I learned something, and heard the little bell."

She looked surprised, then laughed. "I think we've both had enough wine. Let's go back to my place."

Brenda's apartment faced the ocean. A light breeze cooled the room, and the moonlight provided romantic lighting. She fell into Ray's arms. "It's going to get very noisy in your head, because I'm going to teach you a lot of new things tonight," she said, putting her lips to his.

She let her yellow dress drop to the floor, and stood naked in the moonlight. She kissed him again, and when she released him, he too wore nothing, and they settled onto her bed. She took as much as she gave, and only when he fully satisfied her did she surrender herself to his needs, until neither could take nor give any more.

When they were done, sleep did not overtake them.

Ray studied her body in the moonlight. As she lay motionless, he traced his finger over the curves of her body. Teasing her, he watching her lips part and her breath quicken, and didn't stop until her body arched with pleasure.

Again, he did not sleep.

He stared at the ceiling, listening to her breathing, along with the sound of the waves. After a long while she turned to him.

"Did you hear them?" she asked.

"What?"

"The bells. Did you hear any bells?"

"Yes. Sure. A whole orchestra of bells," he said, as he leaned over and kissed her.

"Well, let's see if *this* makes them ring."

"No, not yet. I need another twenty minutes."

She pushed him away. "No, I'm serious," she said, raising herself on one elbow.

"Look at me. What do you see?"

"I see you have no tan lines."

"Well, yes, but what else?"

"I see your beautiful body in the moonlight, and, okay, make that ten minutes."

"Think about what you said. 'Moonlight.' But have you ever *seen* the moon?"

"Huh!"

"That's right. And when you picked me up before, and the sky was the orangey color of sunset, did you *see* the sun?"

"That doesn't make any sense. There must be a moon, and it's just directly overhead."

"Look out the window and look up."

He did as she asked. Silvery moonlight covered everything, yet he could not find the moon in the clear sky. He pulled on his pants and went out. There was no moon, just moonlight. He went inside.

"How is that possible?"

"I don't know, but I noticed it on my first night here. And tomorrow morning you can go out and look for the sun. The sky will look like sunrise, then morning, midday, evening, and sunset. But you won't find the sun."

Ray went to the window and looked up into the clear sky again. "There are stars," he said.

"That's good, when I came here I couldn't see *them* either."

"So you can see them now?"

"Yes, but it took a while. First it was the stars, then the moon. I didn't see the sun for the first time until after I met you."

"What did you think when you did?"

"Nothing really. I'm in a different place now. Why should I expect anything to be the same?"

Ding.

"I think you are amazing," he said, leaning over to kiss her.

She put her arms around him, and amazed him again. When they reached the end of their desire they slept.

Ray smelled eggs and bacon even before he opened his eyes.

"Wake up sleepyhead," she whispered, kissing him gently.

He opened one eye and saw her wearing only a T-shirt. She still looked radiant. During breakfast, Ray stared out the window as he ate. Brenda watched him.

"Yeah, I couldn't figure out how they do it either."

"Who is . . . *are* they?" he asked.

"Management. They run everything, like I said, they make all the rules, assign quests, and stuff like that."

"How do you know that?" Ray asked.

"Since I got here, I get feelings. Not all of the time, but sometimes, and, when I do, my feelings are usually right. Maybe it's like your little bell."

"What are these feelings like?"

"It . . . it's like suddenly understanding something you couldn't figure out before, like suddenly understanding algebra."

"What else have you had feelings about?"

"Mostly personal stuff, like the feeling that I wanted to be with you, even though we would have only a short time together."

"I'm glad for that one, but I never said I was leaving."

"Ray, I know you can't stay here much longer. I'm glad we've had this time together, and we have the rest of the day and tonight, but you have to get back to your quest."

"What if you are my quest?"

"We both know that I'm not, and you know you have to leave the Keys and go where you feel your quest wants you to be."

Brenda's words echoed Rowena's prophesy. He enjoyed his time with her, and now she was telling him he had to continue his quest.

Brenda could see Ray was torn, wanting to stay, but knowing the ways of *The Dim* compelled him to leave.

"Where do you think you will go next?" she continued.

"I wasn't sure, but last night I started thinking about New York. I don't know why, but I think it should be my next destination. But I don't want to leave here yet."

"A guy from New York came into Joe's one night, before you got here. He said he was a professor at some university. He drove down from up north and described his trip the same way you did, the part about it taking so much longer to travel south than west."

"So it wasn't just me. Others have had the same experience."

"Yes, but he had a theory about why," Brenda said.

"What was it?"

"He said it was about the shape of the world. In the other place, the earth is kind of round. Here it's more football-shaped. It's longer from north to south than it is from east to west."

"That could explain it, but it doesn't mean it's true. What else did he say?"

"He said that the seasons would be different too, they would be shorter, and that a day might have a different number of hours, depending on how fast the football . . . er . . . the world spun on its axis."

"That all makes sense, but did he say anything about the missing sun, moon, and stars?"

"Yes. He said they're not missing. He could see them. That kind of freaked me out!"

"But I can't see them," Ray said, and wondered if it was a metaphor for "seeing the light."

"Do you think it could have anything to do with the reason some people are here? Like your quest or my do-over?" she asked.

"Possibly. Did the professor say anything about having a quest or mission or something?"

"I kind of tried to ask, but he didn't want to talk about it. And then he left, and I never saw him again."

"You know, all that thinking has made me tired. Want to go back to bed?"

"How about we take a shower first?"

The next morning Ray was dressed and ready to leave, when Brenda came out of the bathroom wrapped in a pink towel.

"I know you have to get ready for work tonight," he said.

She took him in her arms and kissed him. They held each other silently for a long while. The tugging of his quest, which had been quiet since he arrived at her apartment, began to pull again, and he tried to fight it. He just wanted to stay a little longer. He had found something with her and he didn't want to let go of it just yet. If she was his quest, his journey would be over instead of just beginning.

"I don't want you to go Ray," she said softly, as she pulled only slightly away from him, letting the towel fall to the floor.

"You know I don't want to go," he agreed, and ran his hands over her bare skin.

"If you keep doing that I'll be late for work," she said, sliding out of his embrace and picking up the towel.

"You know I'm going to miss you."

"And you know I have to let you go," she said with an air of certain knowledge.

Ray understood what she meant. But he didn't want to go, and again he was angry at *The Dim*. He was falling in love again, and again he would have to lose the object of his love. He wouldn't ask if she felt the same way. Whatever answer she gave would hurt.

"How long do you think it will take you to get to New York?"

"I'm not sure," he said, without looking at her. "If the professor is right, it could take a week — or longer."

"Good luck on your quest," Brenda said. "And be careful, there are dangers in *The Dim*."

Ray didn't try for one last kiss goodbye, and didn't look back to see if she wanted him to. He hurried out the door and down to the street. He knew if he stayed one minute longer he might never leave.

Chapter 24

It was mid-afternoon when Ray left Brenda. He didn't plan to leave Key West until the next morning. He knew the trip to Miami would be relatively short, but had no idea how long it would take to get to New York, and he didn't care.

He went to the boarding house where JC was staying. A good-looking young man passed him on the stairs as he went up. His smile was telling.

JC, in his boxers, was at the door watching him leave, when Ray came up the stairs.

"Hello, my friend, I hoped we could get together again before I left," JC said.

"That's why I'm here. I'm leaving in the morning."

"Well this is a good thing then. Let us go for a farewell drink."

JC slipped on some shorts and a T-shirt, and in five minutes they were sitting, drinks in hand, at the Tailfin.

"Did you enjoy your time with Brenda?" JC asked.

"Yes, but it was too short. Why is it that in a world where time seems to hold no meaning, there is never enough of it?"

"That is something I cannot answer. I have had the same feeling."

"All I want right now is to tell Donald to take his quest and shove it where the moon don't shine, and stay with Brenda." Ray was almost pleading with JC to grant his wish.

"You know that in all matters we are compelled to follow the ways of *The Dim*. If it were in my power to help you, I would."

"I know," Ray said, staring into space, wishing for that which could never be. "Anyway, it looks like you didn't waste your time."

"Ah, you saw Francois. He is an amazing young fellow. I will be sorry to leave him, too."

Ray noticed the empty look in JC's eyes, and thought it must mirror his own expression. "It seems to be part of the nature of this place that we must constantly be torn from people we become close to," he said.

"And so it is, I think, that we too, must go our separate ways. Have you decided where you are going?" JC asked.

"New York seems to be calling, just a feeling, but in this place that's all the reason anyone needs. And you?"

"If I could, I would return to Haiti, but I still have too many old memories of that place, so I have been told not to return. I think New Orleans will be my next destination."

"Do you have a car?"

"No. A motorcycle. It should not be a long trip. If I leave at sunrise, I should arrive before midnight on the second day. That is when all the good parties start."

"Which leads to my next question. Have you ever seen the stars, moon, or the sun here in *The Dim*?" Ray asked.

JC took a long pause, as if he did not want to admit it. "No."

"Doesn't that bother you?"

"Yes, but I have no way to understand the reason or meaning of it."

"I never noticed, but Brenda asked me if I had ever actually seen them, and I hadn't—until my night with her. Then I saw the stars. She said the same thing happened to her, and thought it was a metaphor of *The Dim*. She said, after a while here, she could see the stars, and sometime later the moon, but didn't see the sun until after we met."

"Perhaps it is that we must learn to see the light. The more we learn, the more we see."

"Judging from your shirt, you should be able to see something tonight."

"It is possible. I will look."

"Another thing I learned from Brenda, it's about this strange north-south travel thing. She met a professor who said this world is probably not round. It's shaped like a football. That's why distances are not what we're used to. It would also affect the seasons and the length of a day."

"That makes very good sense, but why would this world be different in that way?"

"Unfortunately, my friend, I think we may never know the answer."

It was dark when they left the Tailfin. Both men looked up at the night sky. In *The Dim*, they both saw the moon for the first time.

"Does it look different to you?" JC asked.

"The dark areas are different. It . . . it's like . . . no, wait, I've seen satellite pictures. We're looking at the other side of the moon."

"I think you are correct. If so, could *The Dim* be a reflection of the other world?"

"Anything is possible," Ray said. "It will give me something else to think about on the road." He extended his hand. "Good luck my friend."

"*Bonne chance, mon ami*," JC said, taking his hand. "Perhaps our paths will cross again."

Each man had unfinished business here. Ray watched JC walk to the side street where Queen Rowena's bungalow was secluded behind hedges.

Ray wandered down the street toward Joe's. He stood outside watching Brenda working the bar. The same four ladies still held their discussion group at the far end. At the table no longer occupied by Matt and Tony, Smokey and Starla now sat close to each other. Miguel sat alone at a corner table watching everyone.

On his first night here, Ray had sat at the bar, talking to Brenda. It seemed like months ago. In fact, it was only a week in *The Dim*.

Chapter 25

The next morning, Ray was on US1 heading east toward Miami. He should have had to lower the visor to shade his eyes from the glare of the morning sun, but he didn't have to. Again, it seemed to always be just above his windshield. In the other world, it would take twenty-four hours to drive the sixteen hundred miles to New York. In this world, he had no idea how long it would take or exactly how far it was. He found it frustrating that *The Dim* did everything it could to keep him disoriented. Right now he had no idea of the date or even the day of the week. It didn't matter. The one thing he was sure of was that he had no intention of driving sixteen hundred miles on I-95.

He got on the Florida Turnpike just north of Miami and drove north to where it connected to I-75 and continued to the Georgia border. That part of his journey took three days. From there he planned to stay on two-lane blacktop. As long as the compass pointed north or northeast, he would get there — eventually. He made the assumption that north was really north, and if he found it wasn't he would probably hear that damn little bell again. So far his compass was true.

He drove the winding blacktop through swampland, forests of scrub pine, cotton fields, and valleys of farmland rimmed by timeworn mountains. There were some towns, if you could call them that, with a motel, restaurant, and a bar, but not much else. They were outnumbered by the towns that used to be. Decaying buildings overgrown with weeds. Nature's reclamation of what man had abandoned. Ray wondered why such places should exist at all in *The Dim*.

The people he encountered paid as little attention to him as he did to them. The singular commonality in all of the places he stopped was the waitresses. They all had a lot of hair. Some had big, blonde beehives, piled like bales of hay on their heads, others had long ponytails down to their waists. Watching them made him feel uneasy, out of time, out of place.

He had seen the moon nine times by the time he crossed the Maryland state line. The first road sign he saw was "Welcome to Newcomerstown." A sign on another post read: "Main Artery to Town," with an arrow pointing straight ahead. Underneath was another arrow pointing left, and the word "Bypass."

With daylight fading, Ray chose to go straight.

Chapter 26

Trees lined the dark country road leading to town. Ray wondered if he had missed a turn, until he saw a red light ahead in the distance. He continued until the road widened and became Main Street. The distant red light was from a neon sign on the side of a weathered brick building.

Ray studied the sign:

Newcomerstown Blood Bank
We Need Your Support
Please Give

It looked more like a plea for help than a request for donations. He couldn't imagine why blood donations were needed in *The Dim*. He hadn't seen any hospitals or doctors' offices. Yet, on a moonlit night in this strange old town, the red sign compelled him to stop.

He parked in front of the building. There weren't more than a dozen lampposts on the entire length of the street that abruptly ended in darkness after a few blocks. Signs for the Full Moon Motel, and the Night Owl Diner sat opposite each other.

He was tired, and this town had a place to eat and sleep. That was enough. He looked up at the sign on the building again.

Why here?

Then, he remembered Rowena's admonition to give of himself. He didn't know why he should remember that now, and couldn't imagine what he could gain, but again, he had to follow his feelings. He entered the building.

Too few fluorescent bulbs lit the room, which smelled of old wood and alcohol.

"Welcome to Newcomerstown. Have a seat," said a matronly woman with skin as white as her uniform, directing him to a chair next to a desk. She sat and pulled a sheet of paper from a stack.

"Have you donated here before?"

"No."

Have you given blood anywhere else in the past three months?"

No."

"Good," she nodded. "Have you ever had AIDS, hepatitis A, B, or C, or any sexually transmitted diseases?"

"No."

She nodded again. "Very good. Do you take any non-prescription medications or narcotics?"

"No."

"Alright then, you look nice and healthy, so why don't you just sit on that recliner over there, and we can get started."

Ray complied. He started feeling hungry, and had misgivings about making this his first stop in town.

The nurse sterilized the inside of his right arm and inserted a needle connected to a tube leading to a collection bag behind him.

Ray rhythmically flexed the muscles in his arm to hasten the flow of blood. After what seemed like too long an interval, the nurse returned and cheerily announced, "You're done," and removed the needle from his arm, placing a bandage over the puncture.

Ray declined the customary offer of juice and cookies, looking forward to a more substantial meal. He watched the nurse remove the collection bag from the stand and he gasped. "How much did you take?"

"About a pint and a half, but don't worry you still have enough. After a good dinner, you'll feel just fine."

When he felt steady enough to stand up, the nurse slapped a sticker on the front of his shirt. It was red, shaped like an oversized drop of blood, with white letters announcing: "I GAVE."

"Just wear this until you leave town," she said dismissively, and returned to her desk.

Puzzled, Ray looked at her and chose not to ask any questions.

He drove to the motel, checked in, then walked across the street, pausing to look up at the unfamiliar moon. *What the hell?* The moon was full a week ago when he and JC saw it for the first time. It should have been waning, down to three-quarters or less by now. He reasoned the strange looking moon also had a strange orbit.

Crossing the street, he noticed the road and sidewalks were old and broken. He looked around at the other buildings. Most were dark or boarded up. Newcomerstown had long since passed its prime.

A pink and green neon sign hung over the door of the Night Owl Diner.

"Welcome! Come in and have a seat," said the thin man with a paper hat and white apron. He had a thick Eastern European accent.

Nick (according to the name embroidered on his apron) was wiping down the counter until Ray walked in, and his eyes locked onto the "I Gave" sticker.

Ray sat in one of the empty booths, facing the far end of the counter, where two waitresses negotiated the narrow passageway carrying plates to other customers, who gave no notice to the new arrival. Nick brought a glass of water and a menu to Ray.

"I see you already made your donation to our community," he said, pointing to the sticker on Ray's shirt. "We like people who are generous and willing to give something when they come here to enjoy our hospitality. I'll have one of the girls take care of you."

Nick waved for one of them to come over. They both looked at Ray, then, after a pause, one said to the other, "Val, I think he's your type."

Ray watched the raven-haired girl slowly walk down the length of the counter toward him. She pulled an order pad and pen out from her apron pocket and looked at the sticker on his shirt.

Ray liked the way she moved and the way her tongue wet her lips. He was surprised he had enough blood left to feel aroused.

"I'm Val," she said with a sly smile. "The special tonight is a sixteen-ounce rib-eye."

Rays sat with his eyes fixated on her dark eyes and red lips. He also noticed her smile revealed slightly elongated canines. *Ding.*

"Wait a second, what kind of place is this?" he said raising his voice and starting to get up.

Ray suddenly felt the many eyes that now turned toward him.

"Relax, honey, you're safe. That sticker makes you a friend of everybody here."

Ray saw Nick and the other waitress watching him. They smiled and nodded.

Ray slid back down in his seat, still uneasy. The other customers turned back to their plates.

"Do you want it?" she asked.

Ray's mind ran in several directions at once.

"Want what?"

"The rib-eye, silly."

"That. Oh yeah."

"How would you like it?"

"Huh?"

"The steak. How would you like it, rare, medium or well done?" she said rolling her eyes.

"Medium."

"Fries or baked?"

Ray still couldn't get his thoughts together.

"Huh?"

"Your potato, what kind?"

"Fries."

"I'm not even gonna ask what kind of salad you want. I'll just bring something you'll like.

"Uh, could I get a beer with that?"

"No, you need to get your fluids up. Just drink your water, and I'll get you a refill when I bring your order."

Still unsure of what to make of his situation, Ray watched her hips move as she walked his order back to the chef. A few minutes later she returned with his meal. He was hungry and didn't waste any time eating it, downing three glasses of water as well. When Val returned to his table to see if he wanted dessert, he declined and asked for the check.

"No charge for you tonight. Your donation covers it."

"B-u-t-t-t . . . " Ray sputtered.

"You staying at the Full Moon?" she asked.

He nodded.

"Nick, can I take my break now? I want to walk . . . what's your name?"

"Ray."

"Yeah, I want to walk Ray back to his room."

Nick gave her a sly smile. "It's not busy now, but don't take too long, alright?"

"Look Ray, I know this is a lot for you to take in. I'm gonna take you back to the motel."

"You don't have to do this," Ray said, as they crossed the street. "I'm okay, really."

"I know, but it's a nice night to get out for a little walk," she said, taking his arm.

They crossed the street. The full moon provided more light than the antiquated street lamps.

"Room nineteen, that's *my* lucky number," Val said as Ray unlocked the door.

"Look, I appreciate the special service, but you really don't have to —"

"Looks like it's your lucky number too," she said.

She pushed him into the room, kicked the door closed, and threw her arms around Ray, pressing her moist red lips against his.

Thirty minutes later, they both lay naked on the bed, still breathing hard.

"So, I've got to ask you, what's with this town anyway?" Ray said turning to her.

"What do you mean exactly?" she said, raising up on one elbow, and playing with his chest hair with her free hand.

"Well," he hesitated, "you know, the blood bank thing, the funny looks in the diner, and the VIP treatment for having the 'I Gave' sticker?"

"Ray, you already know."

"You mean this is *real*? You . . . you *are* vampires?" He sat up.

"This is *The Dim*. Everything is real and anything can be real," she said.

Ding.

"So, if you are a vampire, what are you doing here? Aren't you supposed to be immortal?"

Suddenly she looked sad, and slumped back on her pillow

"We thought so. We used to be. Except for wooden stakes and silver bullets, that is."

"What about Holy water?"

She turned. "Seriously?"

"Sorry, I wasn't thinking."

"Anyway, back in the fourteenth century something happened. The Black Plague. It contaminated the blood supply. That's when my parents died."

"For a seven hundred-year old woman you sure do have a great body."

She soft punched him on the shoulder.

"Just sayin'."

"Anyway, those of us who survived were okay until the nineteen eighties. People started getting a lot of bad habits then. First AIDS was a problem. I could smell the infected ones a block away. Not everyone could. Then Hep-C and all of the other STDs decimated our remaining numbers. Almost all of the rest of us were killed by drugs — cocaine, crystal meth, Ex. We couldn't sense those until it was too late. There are still some of us left in the other world. They keep the myths and legends alive. Some pass between this world and the other one looking for peace, I guess, but I don't think they'll keep going much longer."

"I'm sorry. I never would have thought . . ." He tried to sound sincere.

"Yeah, so here we found a way to adapt and survive, so to speak."

"The Blood Bank?"

"Exactly. We manage to get enough people, like you, to give voluntarily, so we don't have to feed on live humans, and we get to test the blood first so we don't get sick. It's a win-win."

"But is it the same thing, the taste or whatever you are supposed to get from it?"

"Well, it's like the difference between eating steak or a hamburger. They're both meat, but eating steak is much more . . . *filling*."

"It does make sense, I suppose. But what if you don't get enough donations?"

"Forget about that now," she said and kissed him.

"There is one thing," she said.

"What?"

"Could I take the bandage off your arm?"

"Why?"

"Because there is usually one or two drops of blood left at the needle site, and I just want to taste you, please. It won't hurt, I promise."

"Isn't that dangerous?" he asked.

"It won't make you one of us, if that's what you're afraid of. Please," she said.

It was a simple request, from the beautiful naked woman that lay next to him, *and* she did say please.

"Okay, just be careful."

Slowly, she took the bandage off, and placed her mouth over the wound. He felt her tongue play at the needle site.

When she released his arm, she kissed him again. "Thank you. It was wonderful."

"More wonderful than . . . *before*?" he said, feeling a little light headed again.

She nodded. "But don't get me wrong, before was great. It's just that this is different. I don't know if it will be the same for you. Do you want to taste me?"

"I don't know . . ."

With one, long red fingernail she scratched her nipple. A thin line of red blood surfaced. He should have been repelled, but the sight captivated him the way the red neon sign on the blood bank had.

Val pulled his head toward her breast. He had no will to resist. He put his mouth to her nipple, feeling the warmth of her skin, and then tasted her. She tasted sweet. Then the room seemed to spin. He felt he was at the center of a vortex. Her arms no longer gripped him, but he was unable to pull away. He wanted more. He could hear her heart beating louder and felt the movement of her chest as her breathing quickened. She gave herself to him for as long as he wanted. Still clinging to her and tasting her precious fluid, his mind filled with strange images of ancient places, some violent and frightening, some sweet like the taste of Val. Then, sleep.

Chapter 27

Ray awoke, but didn't open his eyes. He reached across the bed, but felt only the cool sheets. He wasn't surprised Val was gone, only that he hadn't heard her leave. This was the first of several surprises that would greet him today.

He opened his eyes and the only light was the pale gray daylight framing the curtained window. His memory of the past twenty-four hours seemed intact. He sat up and suddenly felt "off." And it wasn't from giving blood. No. It was something else.

He showered, and when he stood in front of the mirror to shave, he noticed the difference. That was his second surprise. He looked older. Not the age he was when he left the other world, but more like a man of fifty than forty. A little less hair, a little more gut. He rubbed the stubble on his chin, and was sure he had been asleep for only one night. He felt time catching up with him and needed to continue his quest—but not before coffee and breakfast.

The safety lock on the door was still in position. Val must have left another way. *Where does a vampire move on to?* he wondered. The Dim *version of Transylvania?* He shrugged off the thought.

Outside something else was different. The sky was a thick, dark overcast, and a heavy rain created deep puddles in the broken pavement. Unlike the sun-showers that blew over the Keys, this rain was cold and heavy, the kind he had not seen since his arrival at The Rest Inn.

With his head down against the rain, he headed toward the Night Owl Diner across the street. At the curb, he instinctively looked left and right before crossing. There were no cars. "What the hell!" he said aloud.

A space between two boarded-up buildings, overgrown with weeds and strewn with litter, was all there was in the place where the diner had been. That was his third surprise.

Ray stood in the rain, his hair falling in wet strands across his face. He looked up and down the street to see if he had misjudged the location. He hadn't. Then he realized that in a town inhabited by vampires, the Night Owl Diner could only exist between sundown and sunrise. *Ding.*

Ray wanted to see Val again, but accepted the fact that she was gone. It was not as easy to accept getting on the road without coffee and breakfast. "Damn!"

He drove ten miles through the downpour on the deserted two-lane blacktop before crossing the state line into Pennsylvania. There he found Mason's Diner next to the Dixon Express gas station. *The Dim* had its own sense of humor.

After a second cup of coffee, Ray, now older and presumably a little wiser than he had been the night before, needed to decide what course of action would take him closer to the end of his quest.

He'd been on the road for over a week. The feelings that first drew him to go to New York persisted. Donald did warn him not to return to places he had a strong emotional attachment to, but also to follow his feelings.

A conflict of principles in *The Dim*. So why then did he have such a strong urge to ignore Donald's warning? Because New York had been the epicenter of the best time of his life, when he was young, for real, and enjoyed a true zest for life. It was where he met Abby and Wendy. Maybe if he went back to the place where he met them he could recapture the excitement and energy of his youth. He chose to let his feelings win this debate, but his resolve would have to endure two more days on the road.

Gary Ader

Chapter 28

It was noon on the third day when he crossed the Verrazano Bridge to Brooklyn and headed for his alma mater on Long Island. His excitement grew, as he got closer. Yes, this was what he needed to get his mojo back.

He drove onto the campus and found a parking space. It was something that could only happen in *The Dim.*

He walked to the front of the library, where he and Abby exchanged spy codes for the first time, and looked at the white, marble facade. He saw the student union on the other side of the quad, where he had met Walt, who became his lifelong friend. Across the lawn, a bench built into a stone garden wall, was where he and Wendy sat and planned their future together. He wanted to sit there again. Those were happy days. He breathed deeply and tried to remember every detail of as many days as he could.

The positive vibe he hoped to evoke did not materialize. The feelings of joy he yearned to recall eluded him. Instead, he was overtaken by a sadness darker than any he had ever experienced. It engulfed him like a black fog. It was the sadness that came from grief he had never taken the time to acknowledge. And now it took him.

In *The Dim* he was alive, and his family was taken from him. It was as if they were dead. He had never thought of it that way before, and now it filled him with an unbearable grief. In the instant of his own death he had lost them all, and he mourned so deeply his knees buckled, and he fell to the ground. He felt as though he would drown in his own tears. The pain in his chest was deep and growing. He still had enough presence of thought to hope that they were really okay, in the other world, and it was he who was dead to them. Then he did something he had never thought possible. He mourned for himself. It was his death that robbed his wife and children of a husband and father. And the pain grew worse. Knowing that he could never be there for them, to give them the comfort, support, and the love he always had, plunged him deeper into the abyss, and he truly wished for the end of his existence.

The pain in his heart was so intense he didn't understand how it could still beat. But it did. With no way to end his suffering, he lay on the ground in a fetal position for a time he could not measure. The pain never abated.

Sensing a shadow over him, he opened his eyes. It was like being under water, looking at a figure beyond the surface. He could not focus at first, but he knew at once who it was.

Donald Spade stood over him, offering neither comfort nor solace. Lacking the strength to beg for help, he tried to cry out, but his throat would not release a sound, and his eyes continued to overflow.

After an immeasurable interval, Donald spoke to him, his tone stern, "I warned you not to return to places with which you had a strong emotional attachment, and even as I gave you that warning, I knew you would disregard it."

Ray's pain eased enough for him to get to his knees. Donald took his arm and helped him to the bench. Sitting in that same space he once occupied with Wendy, deepened his sadness, while his pain diminished enough to comprehend Donald's words, now spoken softly, "You disregarded my warning because it is in your nature to do so. In fact, you were supposed to. What you are experiencing now is a part of your quest. It is for you to decide whether or not to accept the truths placed before you."

Donald discerned a sense of comprehension in Ray's bloodshot eyes. "Now you understand what was truly valuable and most precious in your life. Family, friends, and loved ones are the only things that ever really mattered. Those are the people you should have spent more time with when you could. Instead, you made the conscious choice to follow your patriotic zeal. You made it a part of your self-image, and your being, and inflated its value to fill the demands of your ego. You failed to see that in reality it was of very little value to anyone, except you. You chose your missions over the time you should have been with your family. You know that now don't you?"

Ray nodded silently.

"That young woman you murdered in Paris—"

Ray looked at Donald and shuddered.

"Yes, *murdered*. You can't even deny that to yourself anymore. When you made that choice you set in motion an inevitable chain of consequences. Years later, you chose to drive her grieving father to take his own life. Your guilt for both actions was so deep you carried it beyond the grave into this world. In both cases, there were other choices you could have made, but again, you chose to ignore all other options. It wasn't patriotism that drove you to make those choices, it was your ego."

"But the nuclear treaty —"

"The nuclear treaty would have happened anyway." Donald waved his hand dismissively. "It was meant to happen. The geopolitical climate of the time compelled it to happen, but you were fixated on doing the bidding of others in the name of all holy patriotism. In fact, you went beyond that and took matters into your own hands with malice intent."

Ray now felt a different pain. That which comes after guilt. Remorse. It was like a knife in his back.

"Most of the missions you took so much pride in completing had very little consequence in the time stream that followed."

Hearing these words deepened his pain again. For the first time in his existence, Ray had to face the ugly truths about himself, which went well beyond what he had admitted to JC. He enjoyed the silent pride the ancient Greeks called *philotimo*. He considered his work a noble cause. He paid for that pride with the currency of time, the time he now wished he had spent more wisely with his wife and children. In the balance of his life in the other world, this was a net loss. And now, facing the truths put before him in, he found new knowledge about himself.

Ray thought that returning to this place would enable him to relive the pleasurable emotions of his youth. He was dead wrong. It was the power of his quest, the power of which brought him to the place where Donald could disabuse him, where he would once and for all time, have to face the truth about the actions of his former life. Donald pulled back the curtain and made him look behind it.

Everyone he had met in this world, Darlene, JC, Rowena, and Val, had taught him to see things differently and gain a better understanding of what he so glibly thought of as the "human condition," that which he so audaciously held himself above. They helped prepare him for the wisdom he just gained.

The two men sat on that bench for a long time, long enough for Ray to process the significance of what was happening to him, and to accept these truths as a part of his quest.

"So what happens now?" Ray asked, as his insides began to unclench.

"You are now one step closer to the end of your quest. You have had many experiences on your journey, and each of them has taught you a lesson. Now you have learned an even greater one, and you don't need to hear any bells."

"But what do I do now?"

"You continue to do the things you feel you must. Your time in *The Dim* is growing short, but you are still not ready to move on. Other lessons lie ahead. If you make the right choices, none of them will be as . . . traumatic as this one. I know impatience is part of your nature, but you will do well to take the time to contemplate what you have learned here before you decide what direction to take next. You can get up now and go back to your car. As you move away from this place, your pain will diminish. But the knowledge will remain."

It was getting dark, and the light posts surrounding the library came on. He stood on shaky legs, still in shock from the depth of his emotional ordeal, wiping his eyes as he made his way to the parking lot. He heard Donald call after him.

"We will not be meeting again."

When Ray turned, Donald was gone.

Chapter 29

Of course, Donald was right. Ray's pain and grief did diminish as he distanced himself from that place. By the time he crossed into Manhattan the pain had passed, but his anguish continued, and he was angry.

He was angry with himself, and the world, although he didn't know *which* world. Maybe *all* worlds. In life he had put all of his faith and energy into a cause he never had to justify or explain to anyone: Patriotism. He put his country and his missions first. He believed he had done it for his family, for their freedom. He now felt as though he had worshiped a false god. Donald let him see that for himself. His family should have been the most important part of his life, and he wished the time he spent away from home carrying messages destined for the president could have been spent with them. There was nothing he could do about that now, and with no other outlet, he seethed.

He drove to what he had known as the Algonquin Hotel on Forty-Fourth Street. In *The Dim*, it was the Montauk Hotel. He was given room 1919. Not tired enough for sleep, he left the hotel, to walk and think. The midtown he knew was usually busy until the early hours, but that was in another world. In this one street traffic seemed thin, and for a clear evening, the usual crowds of theatregoers were sparse.

The sky was clear, but in the canyons of concrete lining every block he couldn't see the moon. He walked to Times Square. The cool air refreshed him. He didn't stop at any of the bars and restaurants on every block.

When he reached Central Park, he took the path around to the west side that passed Strawberry Fields. Away from the neon signs of midtown, the streetlights cast shadows of bare tree limbs. A few brown leaves still swirled in the light breeze. Everything seemed familiar, and odd. New York was Ray's hometown, the place he was born and raised, but in *The Dim,* it lacked the texture and energy he remembered from the other world. But he wasn't in the other world anymore. He had to keep reminding himself of that fact. He was in *The Dim, The Dimedium,* the half night. Everything seemed half of what it should have been. The crowds, the brightness of the neon lights on Times Square, all seemed *dim*inished. The only thing that seemed brighter was his self-awareness. His experiences that day had given him a clarity of thought that was both unfamiliar and frightening.

He saw an old man sitting on a bench. Cobwebs seem to hold him in place, and dead leaves settled around his feet, unmoved. The man's eyes followed him as he passed.

Ray stopped and turned. He saw recognition in the old man's eyes. He walked closer. The man was so thin he was almost like a skeleton with skin, and his hair as white as bone.

"Do, I know you?" Ray asked.

"Yes, yes, I think we did meet once, somewhere," he said.

His voice was thin and higher-pitched than Ray thought a man's voice should be. "How long have you been here?"

"I don't kno-w-w-w-w, but it seems like a very long time," he said, dragging out the word know.

"Why are you here?"

"I, I think I have been waiting for someone."

"Who?"

"Yo-o-o-o-u. I think I was waiting for yo-o-o-o-u," he said.

"What? Why would you wait for me? And why here?"

"I don't kno-w-w-w-w," he said.

"I remember you now," Ray said. "We met in a shopping mall in South Carolina. I was minding my own business waiting for my wife, and you came over and started asking me if I read the Bible and believed in God. You really pissed me off."

"Yes, that's right, but you didn't seem angry. You said you didn't believe in those things."

"So how did all of that stuff work out for you?" Ray said, letting some of his anger vent.

"I don't know. It's nothing like I expected."

"You mean you weren't welcomed into the bosom of the Lord? You weren't reunited with all of your lost loved ones?" Ray could not mask his sarcasm, especially after what he had been through today.

"No-o-o-o. That is what I expected, but it didn't happen."

"You mean all of your Bible thumping and praying didn't work?"

"Apparently not," he said, sadness filling his eyes.

"Maybe you were praying to the wrong god. Maybe you should have spent more time enjoying your family and less time in church."

"Do you really think that's true?" he asked.

Ray brushed some of the cobwebs off the bench with his hand and sat next to the old gentleman, who smiled in surprise.

"Yes, my friend I do. I too worshiped a false god. I called it patriotism. I traveled the world for years on missions I believed were protecting our democracy. And you know what? It was all bullshit. The only things that were important were the people I loved. People are the most important things. Nothing else really matters at all. I learned that too late. And now there's nothing I can do about it," Ray said, remembering the pain he felt just a few hours earlier. He wished he could cry again, but he had no tears left. *Ding.*

"I think I understand. When my wife was sick, I spent hours every day in church praying for her. I should have been at her bedside with her and my children. We could have prayed together . . ." He paused. "Did you hear that?"

"What?" Ray asked.

"The bell. I thought I heard a small bell," he said, looking around.

"It was in your head. You just gained wisdom. You realized something you never considered before."

A chill breeze stirred some of the leaves on the ground.

"Yes, I remember now. He said that would happen."

"Who said that?"

"The Teacher. He was very nice, to-o-o-o. He reminded me of my social studies teacher in high school.

He told me I had to learn some things here before I could—what was it was he said?—yes, before I could move on. Do you know what that is?"

"I thought I did, but now I'm not sure. I don't know if it means moving on to another life or if it is just a metaphor for something else," Ray said.

"Since you have been here, I feel like I understand things differently. You still seem kind, and I believe what you said. I think my priorities were misplaced. But now it's too late," he said, looking at the ground in front of him.

"I don't think it's too late."

The old man turned to him. "You don't?"

"No. Everyone here is on some sort of quest. I'm in this world to find knowledge and wisdom."

"Yes, the Teacher said that t-o-o-o-o. Have you found knowledge and wisdom?"

"Yes, sort of. It comes in small pieces usually. Today was different. A mountain of knowledge came down on me today, and it hurt like hell."

"I'm sorry that happened. You know, I think my quest was to wait for you. Now that we have spoken, I know it is so. It is time for me to leave this place."

"Where will you go?" Ray asked.

"I don't know-w-w-w. I'll have to sit here a bit longer to think about that."

"Well, good luck to you, my friend, wherever you go," Ray said, getting up.

"Thank y-o-o-o-u," the old man said, "for helping me to hear the bell."

Ray nodded and turned away. The two men of vastly different beliefs and some new understandings parted ways.

After a few steps, Ray turned back. The old man was gone. Only cobwebs and leaves remained. It sent a shiver through him.

White lights on a building up the path, in the other world, beckoned: "The Tavern on the Green." And it had a bar. Ray quickened his pace.

"Double Johnny Black on the rocks, and make it a long pour," he said, and put a twenty dollar bill on the bar.

Chapter 30

Ray sat at the bar long enough to down half a dozen doubles while staring blankly through the floor-to-ceiling windows at the park beyond. The sparkling white lights on the trees outside did nothing to brighten his mood. It was his roughest day since he arrived in this world. Drinking alone, he recounted all of the things he had lost in *The Dim*. His own life should have topped the list, but technically that happened in the other world. And as long as he was being technical, that's where he lost his first family as well.

In this world he had lost Abby and their children and also their grandchildren, Darlene, Brenda, JC, and Val. But today he had lost something he never thought about: his optimism, and, in a way, his sense of innocence. Although, he was not truly innocent of anything; that much he knew. It was his sense of optimism that he missed most. He always chose to believe that all doors were still open to him, and new adventures that lay beyond them would provide the sense of wonderment he once found so exhilarating.

He still remembered the youthful zest for life he once had; recapturing it was why he came back to New York. Now, the certainty that it remained deep inside him was gone. He truly believed he had possessed those qualities, but today those feelings, and the illusions he had held for so long, were ripped from him and torn to shreds. Now, everything that had been dear to him, including his illusions, was gone. The curtain was pulled back, and he could no longer hide from his mistakes.

He tried to reason his situation, which to him became clearer with each glass he emptied. If his quest was for knowledge, he had certainly found it in the truth of the man he really was, and in the truth of the deeds he had done. These were now a part of him. *Ding*.

But that couldn't be all. Nature abhors a vacuum. If something is taken, something else must fill the void. He had not found that something yet, ergo, he reasoned, his quest was not yet complete. There was still more knowledge he must find; he just needed to figure out where to look. It was the reason he was still here and had not disappeared like the old man, or Abby, or Val. *Ding!*

The fact that he still possessed such crystal clear reasoning, despite the enormous quantity of alcohol he had consumed, surprised him. Unfortunately, his motor responses were not working as well as his logic, and he had a long walk back to the hotel. So, he took his leave.

His feelings told him he needed to leave New York, but left him with the same uncertainty he had had so many times before. Where should he go next?

He made his way along the path toward the lights of Central Park South and Sixth Avenue. Stopping for a moment to get his bearings, he looked up and saw the unfamiliar moon in the western part of the sky. It appeared to be perched atop a tower on one of the tall buildings on the west side. He chose to take that as a sign, and resolved to make his next destination west. But that wasn't a destination, it was a direction. In his present condition he considered that a good start. He would head west, and let his feelings and the will of *The Dim* determine his fate.

Gary Ader

Chapter 31

In the clear, bright, sunless light of day, Ray's selection of direction still seemed like a good choice. He would head west. But not yet. He wanted more time to think. He knew he would never be returning to this place, so he set out to explore parts of the island he hadn't seen before. He knew time was not his to waste, but also he sensed his business here was not yet complete.

Ray stopped shaving so he would not have to look at himself in the mirror. He didn't have to. He could feel himself aging, and his footsteps getting heavier. He could still get around alright, but the spring in his step that he had in Key West was no longer a part of him.

South of midtown, he walked the crosstown streets and connecting avenues in random patterns. His observation on the first night that things seemed half of what they were in the other world remained. Street traffic was light, and there were no yellow taxicabs jockeying for curb space. There were no subway entrances on street corners either. Pedestrian traffic was less dense, and nobody seemed to be in a hurry. Very un-New York.

During the day he took his meals at coffee shops, and, as best he could, tried not to engage in conversation with any of the waitresses. At night, he chose neighborhood bars, the kind where the blue-collar union guys hung out — and people minded their own business.

It was late afternoon on day two, when Ray walked up Fifth Avenue. Where St. Patrick's Cathedral would have been in the other world, another edifice now stood, with gray stone like the cathedral, only without the characteristic arches or spires. And it was taller. The top seemed to rise into the sky. Ray attributed that to his angle of view, or perhaps to the way sunlight reflected off the higher floors. No sign or cast-metal lettering indicated a name or purpose of the building. On its face, only the large numerals two and zero. People entered the building through heavy wooden doors, which the uniformed doorman opened easily. Their expressions were mixed: some apprehensive, some elated, others simply serene. Many were dressed in the height of fashion, others decidedly less so. Ray was in the latter group. He decided to go inside to look around.

When he attempted to pass, the doorman blocked his path. He was a large man, wearing a red coat and hat, and looking like one of the Royal Fusiliers. His well-trimmed, red beard and deep voice made him an imposing presence to some, perhaps, but not to Ray.

"Excuse me," Ray said forcefully.

"I'm sorry sir, this place is not for you," Red Beard said sternly.

"What the hell are you talking about?" Ray said, with his most offensive New York attitude. "I can go in there if I want to, just like everyone else." He pointed to the others.

"I'm afraid not sir," the doorman insisted, glaring at Ray.

"Who's your boss, I want to talk to him."

"Mr. Walker, my boss is Donald Spade. He gave me explicit instructions not to admit you to this building under any circumstances."

Ray seethed. He remembered his last encounter with Donald Spade. He was still angry that Donald hadn't found a different way to impart knowledge to him.

"Who the hell does he think he is anyway, God?" Ray shouted.

The doorman's expression changed. His face turned as red as his uniform. It was as if Ray had spat in his face. Now, he stood as solid as the stone edifice he guarded.

"Sir, you would do well to leave this place at once, and without any further fuss," he said, loudly enough for Ray to feel the pavement tremble beneath his feet.

Having no desire to test the limits of Queen Rowena's protection, Ray chose to withdraw.

He walked back to his hotel and tried to make sense of what had happened, using the logic of *The Dim*. He started with the number twenty on the building. All of the hotel rooms he stayed in were number nineteen. Maybe Donald thought he wasn't ready for number twenty yet. That seemed logical.

The change in the doorman's expression when Ray asked if Donald thought he was God, made Ray remember their first encounter. Ray had asked if there was a God, and Donald had said "No," but that didn't mean there was no higher power. Could Donald Spade *be* the higher power? Had he actually been face to face with the Supreme Being? No, he reasoned, more likely Donald was one of His assistants . . . or, one of *Her* assistants. *Ding! Ding!*

Ray suddenly felt very small. "Holy shit," he said, before realizing he was, more or less, literally correct.

He had seen people going into the building, but no one was leaving. That could be an aberration of the time of day, or was this building a gateway for people moving on? Could the building that occupied the space where St. Patrick's Cathedral stood in the other world be the gateway for those moving on? Apparently, Donald Spade, in his own wisdom, decided that this was not the time for him to receive that knowledge. Enough.

Chapter 32

The following day, Ray had breakfast in the coffee shop next to the Montauk, then got into his car and left New York for the last time. He drove through the Lincoln Tunnel to New Jersey, made his way to Pennsylvania, and got on I-84 westbound.

Just as before, regardless of the time of day, the sun always seemed to be just above his windshield, even when heading due west late in the afternoon. It was as if he were racing against himself. As long as he could not see the sun, his quest was not complete, and he could stay in this world. He had grown used to *The Dim*, in a twisted kind of way, and wasn't ready to begin learning the ways of another world. He had more to do, more knowledge to gain, *and* there was something he could not put a word or name to.

There was something *else*. He thought he might still be under the protection of Queen Rowena. After all, he did walk through Central Park in the middle of the night, drunk, and nothing happened. That was just a theory, one he wisely chose not to put to the test against Red Beard.

Each day, miles of asphalt passed under his tires. His destination lay somewhere beyond the horizon. When he was too tired to continue, there was always a motel and a place to eat. Most of the waitresses asked the same questions, and he gave the same answers.

"Where are you heading?" they would say.

"West."

"That's a big place."

"Yes it is."

"Any place special?"

"No."

At that point the conversation usually ended. As long as his coffee cup or whiskey glass was full, Ray didn't care.

He didn't want any emotional detours on this leg of his journey, and made it a point not to get friendly with anyone. Besides, he had no idea how old he looked now. He hadn't shaved in over a week — or, was it two? He couldn't remember. The growth on his chin was thick. It seemed like a very long time since he left The Rest Inn, and maybe it was. But he had no way of knowing that either. Time was elastic here. He couldn't even be sure how long a day was. He couldn't remember *all* of the places he had stayed, only some. Those were the ones that left him with memories of sadness and loss. The others were just blank spaces in his mind.

After Pennsylvania, the Interstate ended, and Ray continued on two-lane blacktop. Ohio, and Illinois all looked the same in this world. It wasn't until he was half way through Iowa, when the scenery changed — to cornfields as far as the eye could see, in every direction. From Iowa, the blacktop swung north into South Dakota. Rolling hills and distant mountains welcomed him to another land. He was out West, and it was a big place.

One night in a bar, he looked at a map on the wall near the men's room, looking for a destination. Las Vegas and Reno had no appeal for him, not now anyway. The Pacific Ocean states seemed too far away. His destiny must lie somewhere in between.

As he traveled, the days got shorter and the weather cooler. Two thirds of the country was behind him when he crossed the Wyoming state line.

Gary Ader

Chapter 33

On the afternoon of the third day after crossing into Wyoming, Ray arrived in Jackson. A park in the center of town was surrounded by tourist shops, restaurants, bars, and The Peaks Motel. The park had an entrance at each of its four corners. At each entrance stood a twenty-foot-tall arch made of elk antlers, and guarding the entrance was a cowboy with a black hat, holding two six guns. Ray couldn't tell what they were supposed to be guarding in an empty park, but their eyes constantly scanned the arc of space before them.

Ray checked into The Peaks, a three-story building with a roofline contoured to the shape of the distant mountain backdrop. He carried his suitcase upstairs to Room 19. Other than the cowboy décor, it was no different than any of the other places he had stayed; yet this time he felt a vague sense of uneasiness.

Settling into an upholstered chair in the corner of the room he studied the interior. It didn't take him long to realize the only thing that was weird was him. He felt different. He knew that there was a reason for everything he experienced in *The Dim,* and the reason for his uneasiness would eventually manifest itself. In the meantime, he had his own way of dealing with it.

Ray walked to the Million Dollar Cowboy Bar on the other side of the park, passing two of the antler arches and two of the cowboy sentinels to get there. The bar smelled of old wood, whiskey, and beer. Loud music played from a jukebox. The bar stools were saddles mounted on pedestals, and Ray chose one towards the back of the room. On his last two nights on the road he had skipped the bars and gone to bed sober, a possible reason for his vague anxiety. Tonight he needed to make up for lost time. A lanky bartender with a handlebar moustache and a black vest approached.

"What'll ya have cowboy?" he said with a twang.

Ray looked around for the "cowboy," before realizing the bartender was speaking to him.

"Two double Scotches on the rocks."

As he drank from the first glass, he saw his reflection in the mirror behind the bar. His beard was full, and mostly gray, as was the hair on his head. His age in *The Dim* was catching up to the age he was when he left the other world. He took it to mean that he was nearing the end of his quest--but *how* near, or what was at the end, remained unknown.

He was starting his second drink when he noticed an attractive girl at the far end of the bar. Her blank expression reminded him of the woman he had seen at the Tailfin—alone, disoriented, and isolated.

When the bartender picked up the first empty glass, Ray ordered two more. The scent of perfume preceded the approach of a woman, who chose the seat next to him. He guessed she was about his age, give or take a little, which didn't really matter. Her hair was red, her lipstick redder. She had more curves than the slalom at Vail, and he liked the way her ass filled the saddle. Her makeup did little to conceal her age, but she had a warm smile, and smelled good, two things Ray always liked about women.

"You look like a lone wolf sitting here all by yourself," she said.

"If you say so."

"Care to buy a lady a drink?"

"What do you drink?"

"Whatever you're drinking."

Ray, now with three glasses in front of him, pushed one in front of her.

"Thanks. I'm Ann."

"Ray. You live around here?" he asked, realizing the irony.

She laughed. "No. Do you?"

"No. Just got in. Somehow this just feels like the place I need to be."

"I know what you mean. I got in a few days ago, and saw the sunset for the first time in this world," she said, as if they were old friends reminiscing.

"I guess that means you're a short timer," Ray said.

"Maybe. I have no way of knowing. I guess nobody does. Listen, don't take this the wrong way or anything, but you look a little long in the tooth to be riding a filly, if you know what I mean," she said, nodding in the direction of the younger woman who still held part of his attention.

"No. I *don't* know what you mean," he said.

"I mean that sometimes an old mare can get you where you need to go just as well . . ." she said smoothing his shirt collar with her hand, ". . . and maybe I need to get to the same place—but if we're not in a hurry . . . ya know."

"Now I know what you mean," Ray said, pushing another drink in front of her. "We might as well start even."

They finished their drinks and walked around the park to The Peaks, and up to Ray's room.

Ray opened his eyes to the early morning light. Ann sat on the edge of the bed next to him, hair and makeup exactly the way they had been the night before.

"I have to go now," she said softly, running her fingers through his beard.

Ray saw apprehension in her eyes. "Ann, I can't be sure, but from everything I've seen, I don't think you have anything to be afraid of," he said, putting his hand on hers. "And thanks, you were right about the slow ride," he said, hoping to see her smile.

"And I was right about you." She leaned over and kissed him. "You know how to make a mare feel like a filly again."

She stood and smoothed her skirt over her curves. "Good luck, Ray. I hope you find what you need, too . . . you know," she said, before closing the door behind her.

Ray realized he didn't know anything about Ann, but he would miss her kindness. *Ding.*

"Damn that bell!" he said, getting up and going to the window. He watched her cross the street to the park. When she approached the antler arch, a cowboy stepped toward her, touching the brim of his hat with his forefinger. She stopped, and he gestured toward the arch. She looked up at Ray standing at the window. Her expression now resolute, she nodded toward him, then walked through the arch, and disappeared.

"I guess it's her time to move on." Ray said.

He became angry and sad. He flopped onto the bed and buried his head in the pillow that still smelled of her perfume. *Why is it that every time I become attached to a women, she's taken away? Why? How many more times will The Dim punish me?*

Gary Ader

Chapter 34

It was ten o'clock when Ray went out for breakfast at the diner near the park. He looked up at the bright blue, cloudless sky, and did not see the sun. *Shit!* After all he had been through, how much more would he have to learn before he could move on? Of course he had no more of an answer to that question than Ann did a few hours ago. He sensed that his remaining time in *The Dim* must be growing shorter, but that was a relative term in a world where time seems to be elastic. There was no little bell. He walked aimlessly through the streets of Jackson, Wyoming, hoping to find some sign of what was to come. He found none.

Jackson is a small town, and, in two hours, Ray was back at The Peaks. He looked up at the window where he had stood when he saw Ann move on. At least that's what he *thought* had happened to her. He couldn't go back up there now, so he decided to start drinking early instead.

To get from the motel to the bar, he had to walk past two of the arches again. He approached the first one, the one Ann disappeared through, and stopped. The clean-shaven cowboy watched him. Still more than twenty feet away, Ray took a step closer to the arch. The cowboy moved to block his path.

"You know this place isn't for you," he said.

"I just wanted to get a better look," Ray answered. In the face of this new challenge, he felt certain he was no longer under the protection of Queen Rowena.

"Best you be movin' on to wherever you were headin'," the cowboy said, putting one hand on the handle of his gun.

"Or what? You'll shoot me? Go ahead, you moron, I'm already dead."

"Do you remember what it was like when you died?" the cowboy asked. "Do you remember how it felt?"

Ray looked at him. "No. I don't remember anything." Both the question and answer seemed irrelevant.

The Cowboy pushed up the brim of his hat. "Well, I don't want to, but, if I have to, I will shoot you. And, if I do, you will more than remember what it was like. You'll *feel* it and a whole lot more."

The thought terrified Ray. For some reason, he had been spared the pain of death. It was something he never thought about before, and he didn't want to now.

He chose not to test the cowboy. When he passed the arch on the other side of the park the other cowboy gave him a cold stare. When Ray paused momentarily, that cowboy raised his arm just enough to point to the bar, indicating to Ray that he should keep walking, which he did.

Inside, Ray took a seat at the bar and ordered a Sidecar. Another man joined him, with one stool separating them. Ray glanced sideways, and the man nodded. Ray didn't. Losing Ann, and then his run-in with the cowboy had put him in a foul mood. He did notice that the stranger was younger than he was, and also had a full beard, only without the gray

"Just get here?" the man asked.

Ray looked over.

"No."

"I just got in from Chicago," he persisted. "Was on the road for six days."

"Must have been on the two-lane blacktop," Ray said, and took a long sip of his drink.

"Yeah. How'd you know?" He extended his hand. "I'm Jack."

"Ray." And they shook hands. "I've covered a lot of miles on the two-lane blacktop," he said, then turned away.

"Hey, you up for a game of pool?"

"Sure, why not," Ray said, conceding any possibility of finding solitude. He downed the shot and picked up his glass of beer.

The two walked to the one pool table not in use, Jack racked, and Ray took the first shot. It was a good break, with the cue ball banking off the cushion and coming to rest on Ray's side of the table.

"Good break, Ray."

Ray stepped aside, as Jack circled the table trying to decide which ball to target.

"We playing straight or eight ball?"

"Straight," Ray said.

"All right," Jack said, as he chalked his cue. "Eleven in the far corner."

He nailed the shot and two more after that.

"Nice work."

"Where you from, Ray?"

"Lots of places, but I still think of New York as home." Ray called his shot, but the object ball banked off the corner of the pocket.

"I guess it must have been fun growing up in the Big Apple. Chicago was okay, but there's a reason they call it the Second City. Nope, I've been to a lot of places and nothing compares to the action and the women in New York—not even L.A. I was a radio DJ in New York for a couple of years before working my way out west."

Jack took his next shot and one more, before giving the table back to Ray. Ray paused, searching his memory for something from his other life. "You were a DJ in New York?"

"Yeah, back in the sixties."

"Wait, you're Professor Jack?"

Jack smiled.

"You mean the "the professor plays the groove—"

"—that gets you and your baby in the mooood," Jack finished in his booming radio voice.

"Damn," Ray said, "I knew there was something about that voice. Man, you have no idea how many Saturday nights I spent listening to you on WPMR. I was with an old friend and . . ." Ray tried to remember the last conversation he had with Walt, a friend from college. ". . . and we talked about how great those days were."

Jack beamed. "Glad to meet somebody who still remembers. Long before I bought the big one, a new generation moved in, and moved all us radio DJs out. Everything went video, then digital."

"Of course I remember. Everyone who was lucky enough to be around then remembers. That was *real* radio. You and all the other DJs were on live, doing your thing with the music that played out of a million car radios every Saturday night."

"I can't say that it was anywhere near that many, but it was what I loved to do," Jack said.

"There was a place I used to take dates, by the beach, just off the parkway, near a pier —"

"I know," Jack said. "You were just watching the submarine races."

"Yeah, yeah, me and a hundred other cars. We had stereo before there was stereo, because you were on everybody's car radio." Ray and Jack laughed, and told stories of the old days while clearing the table two more times.

"So why did you leave New York?" Ray asked.

"Because, my gray-bearded friend, you and your whole generation grew up and moved on. That's why I had to move on, and my next stop was L.A."

The bar wasn't busy yet, but a steady stream of people came and went, some to drink, others just to have a look around. Ray saw one of the new arrivals give him the once over. Ray returned the look. The tall black-bearded man with angular features and gray eyes headed over to the bar. Maybe he was just another guy wanting a drink and a chance to get lucky, maybe not.

While Ray racked for the next game, he looked up and saw the stranger, now with a drink in his hand, approach Jack on the other side of the table.

"Mind if I join you? Name's Alf," he said, extending his hand.

"No problem. I'm Jack. And this is Ray."

Ray nodded, avoiding the proximity that would have required a handshake.

Jack offered Alf the break. They played another two games before they had enough and went back to the bar.

"You boys ever seen a western sunset?" Alf asked.

"Not yet," Jack said.

Ray shook his head, not wanting to admit to his new friends that he had never seen the sun at all—in *this* world.

"Good, I know a perfect spot not far from town, and I got a cooler of beer in the truck," Alf said.

"I'm in," Jack said. "What about you, Ray?"

Ray, normally wary of strangers, saw no red flags, and several drinks had taken the edge off his earlier mood. He hesitated ever so slightly.

Jack saw Ray's hesitation. "C'mon Ray, weather's great. Join us."

If Alf had been pressuring him, he probably would have refused, but Jack's affability left him little room to decline.

"Sure."

The old pickup had more than a few dents, and was covered in so much mud that Ray couldn't tell what color it was. The three men filled the front seat, and Alf drove north. He knew the access point to an old logging trail that led to the top of the mountain. He pushed the lever on the transfer case into four-wheel drive and floored the accelerator. The old motor roared, wheels spun, and gravel flew, while the rest of the old truck groaned and rattled. Jack and Ray were bounced and shaken as Alf steered around rocks and ruts.

From where the old road ended, they had a five-minute walk to the crest of the mountain. The clear air and bright sky allowed for a spectacular view across a valley to the range beyond. They camped on a grassy slope that descended for a half mile before the tree line of a pine forest that extended across the valley floor and up to roughly the same elevation on the opposite slope.

"So, what's your story Alf?" Ray asked.

"Me? Not much of a story. Always liked bein' close to nature. Used to live in Montana."

"Yeah, but what did you do?" Ray persisted.

"Same as you, my friend. I survived, or tried to. I lived off the land, roaming the woods, enjoying nature. One day I got shot by a hunter. End of story."

"Did you have any family?" Jack asked.

"Yes, I did. They were with me when I went down. It still hurts thinkin' about that now."

"What about you, Jack?" Alf asked.

"Well, when I wasn't working, I used to do a lot of camping in Colorado and Arizona. I liked to run through the desert or along rivers."

"So what happened?" Ray asked.

"I was camping with my girlfriend in the Grand Canyon, the east end. I got up one morning and went for a jog along the river. I think my heart gave out. I don't really remember much, just a pain in my chest and hitting the ground. Must have scared the crap out of her. We were a day's hike from the nearest ranger station."

"What about you, Ray?" Alf asked.

"Shit. I bought it on the Interstate. Cut in front of a semi in a rainstorm, trying to make it to an exit ramp." He took another drink of beer. "I guess I *did* make an exit," he laughed. "Thing is, when I was listening to Jack, I remembered that I used to run, too—5Ks, 10Ks mostly—but I did do a half marathon once. When I got older, I kept going, a lot slower, but I could still do the distance."

They sat in silence for a long while, watching the shadows get longer.

Ray leaned back and let his eyes lose focus in the azure sky. He started remembering the people he had met on his journey, and how he learned something new from each of them. In the other world he had met many people, but had only gotten to know a few. He was different now. He took a greater interest in the people he met.

At The Rest Inn he had not been able to accept his new reality. Abby returned to *The Dim* to convince him that his life in the other world had ended. But that wasn't all. When they were young, in the other world, circumstances moved their lives in different directions. She had promised him they would be together in another lifetime. When her promise was kept, she moved on.

In Key West he met several people whose destinies had intersected with his.

Brenda was an amazing woman, damaged by the cruelty of people she trusted in the other world, it was *The Dim* that allowed her to be the person she wanted to be. She said she had not seen the sun in this world until after she had met him. She found happiness there, enjoying sunsets, working at Joe's, and meeting people, like Ray, to share her kindness with. She had found contentment. He wished he could have stayed with her. Only his quest prevented it.

JC and Ray quickly became friends. They had many things in common, including a need to see the truth, in others and in themselves. He had taken Ray to Queen Rowena. She had sequestered herself from the world, thinking there was no one left who would believe in her powers. In Ray, she found someone willing to accept her magic and the truths she revealed.

JC carried a terrible burden of guilt, the consequence of an act of bravery and humanity. One night, he and Ray shared their stories of guilt. Ray convinced him that despite the tragic consequences of that dark night in Haiti, JC had done the only thing he could do: save the life of a young woman. The next day, JC no longer carried the mark of his guilt, and was able to continue his journey, or move on. Ray would never know which.

But there was more. After JC told his story, Ray felt compelled to reveal his own dark secret, after which JC forced him to see the truth he had hidden from for more years than could remember. He did have a choice, and he made the wrong one. Altruism and pride were the shields he used to hide behind from the inevitable and undeniable facts he never dared to face. He wasn't a soldier vanquishing an enemy in battle. He murdered a young woman in cold blood. JC forced him to see that it was his ego that blinded him to the horror of his deed, and the choice he should have made that night in Paris.

Later, Donald made him see the consequences of that truth, and of his secret life.

One night, in the middle of nowhere, the two-lane blacktop road led him to Newcomerstown. Val was the woman who tested his ability to believe in the unbelievable. She was a creature of the night, a centuries-old vampire, and he trusted her with the most valuable parts of his body, letting her drink from his wound.   In Ray, she found a man willing to do something no other man would: satisfy one of her primitive instincts by entering her realm and accepting what she needed to give him — her blood — from the part of her body that nurtured new life. Then she vanished.

He remembered the nameless old man in Central Park, who said he was waiting for Ray, and after their conversation, thanked him for helping him to hear the little bell. And he moved on.

In Jackson, he met Ann, a young woman, gentle and kind, trapped in an old woman's body. Ray liked her for her kindness and inner beauty. She needed someone to appreciate her for who she was, and to return her kindness. Then she moved on.

And now he was with "Professor Jack," a man who had known greatness, before time and life passed him by and relegated him to the history books. Ray reminded him, in a very special way, of the lasting impact he had made on a generation of young radio listeners.

With dazzling brightness, Ray suddenly had the realization that his quest was not only to learn about himself, but also to use the knowledge and wisdom he gained to help others find what they were looking for. He had to understand other people's needs and to give of himself the physical or emotional quality that was missing in their existence. It was his *raison d'etre* in *The Dim.* His quest for knowledge and wisdom was a give-and-take proposition. Gazing blankly into the sky on a hilltop in Wyoming, Ray Walker transcended wisdom and found enlightenment. No little bell this time. He no longer needed to hear it.

Alf spoke. "You know, I'll bet the three of us could run down this hill, through the forest, and clear up to the other ridge."

"In my dreams," Jack said. "I think if I tried that now I would have another heart attack."

"Ray?" Alf asked.

"That would be awesome if I could do it, but do you see all this gray? I probably wouldn't make it to the tree line. Besides, it's getting late. The sun will be setting over that far ridge—"

The sun!

He sat in silent awe. Seeing the sun for the first time since he left the other world filled him with emotion. Tears rolled down his cheeks and his lower lip trembled.

It's okay buddy," Alf said, without looking directly at him. "You've been through a lot on your journey here, but it's almost over. All you have to do is to make it to the tree line."

Ray accepted what Alf said. He had no reason to question him or ask how he knew. It was the way of *The Dim*. He knew there was nothing else he had to give or take in this world. With the same sense of apprehension he had seen in Ann's eyes, he resolved to move forward and run down the hill with Alf.

"Jack, you goin' to join us or what?" Alf asked.

"Sure. Why not?" Jack shrugged, still looking out over the valley, and oblivious to the interchange between Ray and Alf. "What's the worst thing that can happen?"

As the sun began to disappear behind the distant ridge, the full moon made its ascent in the opposite sky. Its strange markings were now familiar to Ray. He felt restless. His skin itched and his joints tingled. He stood up and began pacing back and forth. The last remaining light of day came from the now hidden sun still lighting a sliver of sky above the far ridge. The shades of green in the valley had now turned to gray, as the full moon robbed the colors from the landscape, leaving only black and white.

He felt Rowena's words stir inside him:

"Many of the things you did not accept as real, things that were the stuff of myth and superstition . . . you must accept as real . . . The fabric between the two worlds is very thin in some places . . . the images are fuzzy and dark . . . two lines branch off the first . . . On one path you may find what you have wanted all along, on the other, you must move on . . ."

Alf stood and started stretching his long limbs, as Jack moved restlessly, stretching muscles that had been idle for too long.

"Let's go!" Alf said, starting down the hill, slowly at first, picking up speed, as he got closer to the trees. Ray and Jack followed. In the dusk, three men descended into the valley. Ray felt his heart pounding, and he could hear Jack breathing hard just behind him. The tree line looked like a black wall, but, once they penetrated it, their eyes quickly adjusted. Alf, in the lead, ran between the pines, dodging fallen branches, and jumping over rocks. Ray and Jack followed, veering left and right around obstacles, never losing sight of Alf.

The thin light of the moon now penetrated the forest canopy, and Ray saw the glowing outlines of the terrain. The air was cooler. His breathing became rhythmic, and he felt like he could run forever. He heard Jack behind him, easily keeping up the pace, and no longer gasping for air. Alf ran even faster, and was far ahead of them.

Ray stopped thinking about his breathing and his footing. His attention was now drawn to the smells of the woods, the moist earth, and the pine needles that carpeted this part of the forest. He could hear small animals scurry out of his path. He smelled deer off to his right, and heard them fleeing. Jack was now running even with him on his left, and they ran even faster, closing the distance between themselves and Alf.

As Ray ran, he felt all of the things holding him to *The Dim* begin to vanish. Guilt, fear, loneliness, and anger left him. As they did, he became lighter, and his vantage point changed. He now viewed the wolves from above. He was apart from them now, and watched them clear the tree line, and join the pack on the far ridge.

Time in *The Dim* is elastic, and Ray Walker had no way of knowing he had been there almost as long as he had lived his first life.

His attention turned toward the sky. The essence of that which was once known as Ray Walker, now existed as a sphere of energy, a white light hovering between earth and sky. His attention was drawn upward. The direction of his journey, now as it had always been, was his choice.

Another sphere of white energy approached.

"Hi, Dad."

"Jennifer?"

"Yes, it's me. I've missed you so much."

"Me, too."

The two orbs of energy touched and their white light became brighter.

"Dad, I guess there are some things I need to tell you."

"Yes, and there is much I need to tell you, too. We will have all the time we need now."

"Where are we going?"

"See that tiny point of light, just to the right of the North Star?"

"It looks so far. Does it have a name?"

"I don't think so. When we get there, you can name it."

Together they began their journey into the cosmos, rising slowly at first. Once clear of the atmosphere, they traveled at the only speed they could—the speed of light—but even at that rate, it would take many Earth lifetimes for them to reach their destination, and of course, there would be many adventures along the way.

About the Author

Gary Ader was born and raised in New York City, where he received his Bachelor's Degree from Adelphi University. He has enjoyed a multi-faceted career, working both in private industry and for the federal government, and also as a private consultant.

As a Certified Travel Consultant, Gary worked in the travel industry for over twenty years, mostly as the owner of several retail travel agencies. He has traveled to exotic locations around the world, and has escorted many groups of travelers to some of those destinations. He also operated other retail businesses for over a decade.

Mr. Ader also taught sales and customer service as part of the adjunct faculty of Florida Atlantic University. He has lived in New York, the Washington DC area, Florida, and North Carolina (his present home). This is his first novel.

www.ingramcontent.com/pod-product-compliance
Lightning Source LLC
Chambersburg PA
CBHW020117180626
46812CB00006B/2639